9/16

# CHARLY'S EPIC FIASCOS

Also by Kelli London

*Boyfriend Season*

*Uptown Dreams*

*Boyfriend Season: Cali Boys*

*The Break-Up Diaries, Vol. 1* (with Ni-Ni Simone)

Published by Kensington Publishing Corporation

# CHARLY'S EPIC FIASCOS

## KELLI LONDON

Dafina KTeen Books
KENSINGTON PUBLISHING CORP.
http://www.kensingtonbooks.com

DAFINA KTEEN BOOKS are published by

Kensington Publishing Corp.
119 West 40th Street
New York, NY 10018

All Kensington titles, imprints and distributed lines are available at special quantity discounts for bulk purchases for sales promotion, premiums, fund-raising, educational or institutional use.

Special book excerpts or customized printings can also be created to fit specific needs. For details, write or phone the office of the Kensington Special Sales Manager: Attn. Special Sales Department. Kensington Publishing Corp., 119 West 40th Street, New York, NY 10018. Phone: 1-800-221-2647.

KTeen Reg. US Pat. & TM Off.
Sunburst logo Reg. US Pat. & TM Off.

ISBN-13: 978-0-7582-6358-2
ISBN-10: 0-7582-6358-9

First Printing: September 2012
10  9  8  7  6  5  4  3  2  1

Printed in the United States of America

*Tweet*
*Chief*
*Geronimo*

*Because*
*there's*
*only*
*one*
*way*
*to*
*make*
*your*
*dreams*
*come*
*true:*

*You*
*have*
*to*
*be*
*true*
*to*
*yourself*
*and*
*make*
*them.*

*This is dedicated to the memory of the other Charlie in*
*my life:*
*Charlie Moffitt,*
*one of the greats*
*who always accepted me*
*and never discouraged me.*

*You are truly missed.*

# Acknowledgments

To my fantastic trio of superheroes who make my world go 'round and life a true joy to live: T, CII and K.

To the world's most loving and priceless and supportive mom (my mom)!

My family and friends: you know who you are and how much you mean.

R.M. Johnson: you are the greatest.

Travis Hunter: thank you.

Selena James: thanks for being there and for our endless talks and mind-storming sessions. English majors rule!

For my readers: As always, I truly and humbly thank you with all of my heart. You're incredible and appreciated.

And for you, *insert your name here*, I thank you for all your support, for reading <u>all</u> of my books, and being the dedicated reader you are. You are truly the best and so amazing.

## From Kelli

As you know by now, I usually have a lot to say. Things such as the following:

- ❤ Be the best you that you can be.
- ❤ Follow your dreams.
- ❤ There's nothing you can't overcome.
- ❤ You can achieve it if you believe it (or something like that. That one sounds borrowed, but my message has been the same. J)!
- ❤ Love interests (read: boys) come and go, so love yourself first.
- ❤ Oh . . . borrowing from the above Love Interest bullet: Love yourself. Trust yourself. Believe in yourself . . . etc., in yourself. You get it.

And while I have advised the above and truly believe that you should follow all of it because you are truly wonderful and worthy of everything positive and beautiful, this time the greatest advice I can give you will be spoken and painted through Charly. Charly is the epitome of a person who knows what she wants and will stop at nothing to get it. I'm afraid that's all I can say, as I don't want to give away the story. However, the good thing is you don't have to wait too long to find out the rest. Just turn the page. ☺

Take care. Be strong. Love yourself.

Your girl,

Kells

Kellilondon.com

Facebook.com/KelliLondon

# I

## EPIC TRUTHFUL LIES

# 1

―――――――

*This is going to be easy. Simple.* "Turn. Turn. Turn!" Charly said, grabbing her little sister, Stormy, by the forearm. She shoved her hip into Stormy's side, forcing her thin frame to round the corner of the schoolyard. Her feet quickened with each step. They were almost home-free.

"Ouch!" Stormy hissed, cradling her torn backpack to her bosom like an infant in an attempt to prevent her books from falling onto the cracked sidewalk. "All this for Mason? Serious? Let go of my arm, Charly. Let me go. If I had known we'd be up here mixed up in drama, I wouldn't have come to meet you. I need to get home and study."

Charly rolled her eyes. Being at home is exactly where her sister needed to be. She hadn't asked Stormy to meet her. In fact, she remembered telling her not to come. She'd had beef with one of the cliques over nothing—not him, as Stormy thought. Nothing, meaning the girls were hating on Charly for being her fabulous self and for being Mason's girl. She held two spots they all seemed to want but couldn't have. She was the It Girl who'd snagged the hottest boy that had ever graced her town. "Go home, Stormy," she said, semi-pushing her sister ahead.

"Do it again and I'm going to—" Stormy began.

"You're going to go home. That's all you're going to do," Charly said matter-of-factly, then began looking around. She was searching for Lola, her best friend. If she had to act a fool, she'd prefer to show out with Lola around, not Stormy. She had to protect her younger sister, not Lola. Lola was a force to be reckoned with and she wasn't afraid of anyone or anything.

A crowd came her and Stormy's way, swarming around them as the students made their way down the block. A shoulder bumped into Charly, pushing her harder than it should have. Charly squared her feet, not allowing herself to fall. Quickly, she scanned the group, but was unable to tell who the culprit was. "If you're bad enough to bump into me while you're in a group, be bad enough to do it solo. Step up," Charly dared whoever.

Stormy pulled her as some members of the crowd turned toward them. "Come on, Charly. Not today," Stormy begged. "Remember the school said if you have one more incident you'd get suspended."

Charly grabbed Stormy's arm again, preparing to jump in front of her in case the person who pushed her stepped forward.

"Hey, baby," Mason called, pushing through the crowd.

"Everything good?" he asked, making his way to her and Stormy. "Or do we gotta be about it?" he asked, then threw a nasty look over his shoulder to the group. " 'Cause I know they don't want that." His statement was a threat, and everyone knew it. Just as Charly was protective over her sister, Mason was protective over her. His lips met her cheek before she could answer him.

"We're fine, Mason," Stormy offered.

Mason nodded. "Better be. They're just mad 'cause they're not you. But you know that. Right?"

Charly smiled. Yes, she knew.

"Good. Listen, I need to run back into the school for a minute," he said, reaching down for her book bag.

Charly hiked it up on her shoulder. "You can go ahead. We're good. I promise."

He stood and watched the crowd disperse and start to thin before he spoke. "All right. I'll catch up to you two in a few." He disappeared into the crowd of students still on school grounds.

"So really, Charly? You were going to fight whoever over him?" Stormy asked again.

Charly ignored the question as she focused on parting the crowd. They needed to get down the block.

"Hey, Charly! Call me later. There's something I want to talk to you about," a girl shouted from across the street.

Charly looked over and nodded. She couldn't have remembered the girl's name if she'd wanted to, let alone her number. Obviously the girl knew her though, but who didn't?

"Catch up with me tomorrow," she answered, then released her grip on Stormy and sucked her teeth at her sister's questioning. Stormy had no idea. Mason was the new guy around and the guy of her dreams. They'd been dating, but she couldn't let him know just how much he had her because then she'd be like every other girl in their town. And she refused to be like the others, acting crazy over a guy.

"Mason, Charly? That's what this is all about?" Stormy asked again.

"Shh," Charly said, shushing her sister. "What did I tell you about that? Stop saying his name, Stormy."

Stormy shook her head and her eyes rolled back in her head. "Serious? What, calling his name is like calling Bloody Mary or something? I *so* thought that Bloody Mary thing only worked with Bloody Mary's name and Brigette's generation. Who believes in such stuff, Charly? You can call anyone's name as many times as you like."

Charly got tense with the mention of their mother. Brigette refused to be called anything besides her given name, and Mom, Mommy, and Mother were definitely out of the question. That she'd made clear. On top of that, she insisted her name be pronounced the correct *French* way, Bri-jeet, not Bridge-jit.

"Please don't bring her up. My afternoon is already hectic enough. I don't wanna have to deal with Brigette until I have to," Charly said, her quick steps forcing rocks to spit from the backs of her shoes. "Just c'mon. And, like you, I need to get my homework done before I go to work. Mr. Miller said if my math assignment is late one more time, he'll fail me. And I can't have that. Not right before we go on break for a week. And I don't want to do any sort of schoolwork while we're out. Oh!" She froze.

A dog ran toward them at top speed from between two bushes, then was snatched back by the chain leash around its neck. It yelped, then wagged its tail, barking. Charly, a little nervous, managed strength and pushed Stormy out of harm's way. Looking into the dog's eyes, she was almost afraid to move. She'd distrusted dogs since she was five, when her mother had convinced her they were all vicious, and now her feelings for them bordered on love/hate. She'd loved them once, and now hated that they made her uncomfortable, but was now determined to get over her fear. A pet salon near her home was hiring, and, whether she liked dogs or not, she needed more money for her new phone and other things.

The wind blew back Charly's hair, exposing the forehead that she disliked so much. Unlike Stormy, she hadn't inherited her mother's, which meant on a breezy day like today, her forehead looked like a miniature sun, a globe as her mother had called it when she was upset. On her mom's really peeved days, which were often, she'd refer to Charly as Headquarters. Charly smoothed her hairdo in place, not knowing what else to do.

Stormy grabbed her arm. "C'mon, Charly. We go through this at least twice a week. You know Keebler's not going to bite you, just like you know he can't break that chain." She shrugged. "I don't know why you're so scared. You used to have a dog, remember? Marlow . . . I think that's the name on the picture. It's in Brigette's photo album."

Charly picked up speed. Her red bootlaces blew in the

wind, clashing against the chocolate of her combats. Yes, she'd had a dog named Marlow for a day, then had come home and found Marlow was gone. Charly had never forgotten about her, but, still, she'd believed her mother then, and now couldn't shake the uneasiness when one approached. Especially Keebler. He'd tried to attack her when he was younger, and she still feared him. So what if he'd gotten old? Teeth were still teeth, and dog's fangs were sharp. "How do you know he won't bite, Stormy? You say that about every dog."

Stormy laughed, jogging behind her. "Well, Charly. Keebler's older than dirt, he doesn't have teeth, and that chain is made for big dogs, I'm thinking over a hundred pounds. Keebler's twenty, soaking wet. What, you think he's going to gnaw you to death?"

Charly had to laugh. She'd forgotten Keebler was minus teeth. "Okay. Maybe you're right. We only have two more blocks," she said, slowing her walk. Her pulse began to settle when she caught sight of the green street sign in the distance, and knew she'd soon be closer to home than barking Keebler. "Only two more and you can get to your precious studying, nerd," she teased Stormy, who laughed. They both knew how proud Charly was of Stormy's intelligence. Stormy didn't hit the books because she needed to; she had to, it was her addiction. "And I can knock out this assignment," she added.

"Yo, Chi-town Charly! Hold up!" Mason called, his footsteps growing louder with each pound on the concrete.

Charly picked up her pace. She wanted to stop but she

couldn't. Boyfriend or not, he had to chase her. That's what kept guys interested. Stormy halted in her tracks, kicked out her leg, and refused to let Charly pass. "What's going on now? Why are you ignoring Mason? Oops, I said his name again." Stormy sighed, pushing up her glasses on her nose.

Charly rolled her eyes. "I'm not really ignoring Mason, Stormy. Watch and learn—I'm just keeping him interested," she said, failing to tell her sister that she was trying to come up with an explanation for disappearing the weekend before. She'd told him she was going to visit her family in New York, and now she just needed to come up with the details. Her chest rose, then fell, letting out her breath in a heavy gasp. What she'd hoped to be a cleansing exhale sputtered out in frustration. "He may be a New Yorker, but we're from the South Side of Chicago. I got to keep the upper hand." She repeated the mantra she used whenever she had to face a problem, but it was no use. The truth was, yes, they had been born on the South Side of Chicago, but now they lived almost seventy miles away from their birthplace in an old people's town. She couldn't wait to leave.

Mason's hand was on her shoulder before Charly knew it. She froze. Turning around was not just an option; she had to. She knew that he knew that she'd heard him now. Summoning her inner actress, she became the character she played for him. Charly switched gears from teenage girl to potential and future Oscar nominee. She erased the glee of him chasing her down from her face and became who and what he knew her to be. Cool, calm, self-assured Charly—the girl who seemed to have it all. Seemed being the operative word since she lacked teen essentials like the Android phone she was saving for and a computer.

"Hey! I said hold up. Guess you didn't hear me. Right?" His voice was rugged and his words seemed final, as if he had nothing else to say. His tone spoke for him. It was sharp and clipped, yet something about it was smooth. Just hearing him speak made her feel good.

She smiled when she turned and faced him. "Hi, Mason. I'm sorry. There's so much wind blowing that I couldn't hear you."

Mason smiled back and did that thing with his eyebrows that made her melt every time. He didn't really raise or wiggle them, but they moved slightly and caused his eyes to light. "Yeah. So . . ." he began, then quieted, throwing Stormy a *please?* look.

"Okay. Okay. Personal space. I get it," Stormy said, then began to walk ahead of them. "You high schoolers are sickening."

Mason smiled at Stormy's back, and Charly grimaced behind it. She hadn't asked Stormy to give her and Mason alone time, and wished that her sister hadn't. The last thing she wanted was to be alone with Mason because every time she was, her lies piled. They'd stacked so high that now she couldn't see past them, and had no idea how to get around or through them.

"So, I've been trying to catch up with you to see how New York was last weekend when you went to visit your pops. You did fly out for the weekend, right?" he asked, his eyes piercing hers like he knew she hadn't gone.

She scrunched her brows together. It was time to flesh out her partial untruths. She thought of her semi-truths that way because to her they were. She'd done and been and imagined it all in her head, so, in a way, her not-so-trues were kind-of-trues.

"Uh, yeah." *Here comes the hook*, she thought while she felt the fattening lie forming on the back of her tongue, pushing its way out her mouth. "Right. But it was no biggie. I wasn't even there a whole two days. I was in and out of Newark before I knew it. I visited my dad and my aunt. She works for a television station—where they film reality shows. One day I'm going to be on one. That's the plan—to become a star."

"Newark? That's Jersey. I thought you said you were flying into Queens." He looked at her, pressing his lips together. He'd totally ignored her star statement.

"Queens? Did I say Queens?" *Dang it*. She shrugged, trying to think of a cover.

"Yep. You said your pops was picking you up at La-Guardia airport. That's in Queens. Guess Newark was cheaper, huh?" He waved his hand at her. "Same difference. Me and my fam do it too. Sometimes it pays to fly into Jersey instead. It's about the same distance when you consider traffic time instead of miles."

Charly nodded, pleased that Mason's travel knowledge had saved her. "Yeah. I know that's right. And I got there when traffic was mad hectic too. I'm talking back to back, bumper to bumper. But it was cool though. Manhattan's always cool, Brooklyn too," she lied about both. She'd never been to Manhattan and she was only five when she'd visited Brooklyn. But she'd gone to places like Central Park and Times Square all the time in her mind, and a mental trip to the Big Apple had to count for something.

"Brooklyn, yeah, it's cool. Matter fact, I miss home so much, I just got a puppy and named her Brooklyn." He smiled.

Charly raised her brows. "Really? That's hot. I just love dogs. In fact, I just applied for a gig working at the pet salon." Another partial lie. She had planned on applying, she just hadn't had time yet.

Nodding in appreciation, his smile grew. "That's good, Charly. And it couldn't have come at a better time." He took her book bag from her, then slung it over his shoulder. "Dang. This is heavy. What'chu got in it?"

"Math," Charly said. "I got to ace this assignment, so I brought home my book and every book the library would let me check out to make sure I get it right. Because I go to New York so much, I kind of fell behind on the formulas," she added. She couldn't have him think her anything less than a genius.

Mason nodded. "Good thinking. Knock it out from all angles. Math is the universal language. Did you know that?" he asked, but didn't give her time to answer. "Let's walk," he said, clearly not letting up. "It must be nice to have your pops send for you a couple times a month. So what'd you do all weekend? Party?"

She kicked pebbles out of her way, wishing they were her lies. She hadn't seen her father since she was five, and it was something that was hard for her to admit, especially since Stormy's dad was still on the scene for birthdays and holidays. The truth was she had no idea where her father was, so she imagined him still living in New York, where she'd last seen him.

"So did you party?" Mason repeated.

*Me, party? Yeah, right! My mom partied while I worked a double to save for a new phone. Then I sat holed up in the house on some fake punishment.* "Yeah, actually I did. Nothing big though. It was a get-together for my aunt. You know, the one I told you about who's a big shot at the network. Well, she just got promoted, and now she's an even bigger big shot. She's got New York on lock."

Mason nodded, then slowed his pace as Charly's house came into view. "That's cool, Charly. Real cool. It's nice to finally have a friend I can chop it up with. Ya know, another city person who can relate. Somebody who gets where I'm from. Not too many people around here can keep up with my Brooklyn pace," he said, referring to the almost-dead town they lived in. Their tiny city was okay for older people, but teens had it bad. They lived in a nine-mile-square radius with only about twenty-five thousand other people. There was only one public high school and one emergency room, which equated to too small and everybody knowing everyone else and their business. Nothing was sacred in Belvidere, Illinois.

Charly took her book bag from Mason. "Trust me, I know. They can't keep up with my Chi-Town pace either. I'm getting out of here ASAP."

He walked her to her door. "Speaking of ASAP. You still gonna be able to come through with helping me with my English paper this week? I have to hand it in right after break, so I'd really like to get it finished as soon as possible. Don't wanna be off from school for a week and have to work." He shrugged. "But I know you're pressed with school and getting an A on the math assignment. Plus, with flying back and forth to New York to check your pops, and trying to work at the pet salon, I know you're busy. But I really need you, Charly," he paused, throwing her a sexy grin that made her insides melt. "I don't even know what a thesis statement is, let alone where one goes in an essay."

Charly smiled, then purposefully bit her tongue to prevent herself from lying again. She'd forgotten when Mason's paper was due. An essay she would be no better at writing than he would. She sucked in English, but couldn't pass up the opportunity to be close to him. "I gotta work tonight and pretty much all week," she said. She was finally kinda sorta truthful. She did have to work. Now that she was sixteen, and had snatched up a job at a local greasy spoon—and, hopefully, the pet salon she'd told him she had applied at—it was up to her to make sure that the electric and cable bills were paid, plus she had to pay for her own clothing. "We've been *very* busy at work, for some reason."

"Okay." Mason grimaced, then looked past her, apparently deep in thought. He rubbed his chin. "I don't know what I'm going to do now. I gotta pass this class. . . ."

Charly pressed her lips together. She couldn't let him down. It was because of her that he'd waited so long to tackle the paper. She'd told him not to worry, that she had him, that she was something like an A or B English student. Now, it'd seem as if her word was no good, and she couldn't have that.

"Kill the worry, Mason. I'll work it out."

# 2

"Charly!"

Before the front door closed behind her, Brigette's voice ambushed her from somewhere inside the house. Probably upstairs in the bedroom, Charly assumed. Ninety-nine-point-seven percent of the time that's where her mother took up residence. Brigette's wide hips were either spread out on the bed or else swishing down the staircase toward the kitchen, where she kept up with her never-ending caloric intake. "Charly! *Char-lee!* Is that you? Don't you hear me talking to you, girl? Stormy was in here thirty minutes ago. Where've you been? Hunh? If you had time to waste, you better have used some of it to pay cable. *Did* you pay the cable bill? All the stations aren't coming in—it's nothing but static on the flat screen. And I gotta record my vampire flick and soaps, you know that."

Charly exhaled, closed the door, and dropped her

heavy book bag on the floor. She hiked her shoulders, flexing her muscles until they tightened, then released them. She was trying to force her blades to relax, which wasn't such a good idea. It was really an oxymoron, as Stormy had pointed out many times, because you couldn't force and relax at the same time.

"Smile. Smile. Smile," she told herself, trying to make herself feel happier so that Brigette wouldn't accuse her of having a disrespectful tone. She couldn't speak to Brigette if she allowed her true emotions to surface. "Ma'am?" she called out, lightening her voice so it wouldn't reflect the you're-already-getting-on-my-nerves attitude she had.

Five raps sounded at the front door, followed by a short pause, then three more knocks. *Lola.* Charly's best friend was making her usual appearance, announcing herself with the sound of eight, the amount of letters in her full name. Lola Dowl, no middle name or initial.

"Ma'am? Don't ma'am me when I'm calling you, Charly. Get your grown butt up here and help me slip into this girdle!" Brigette yelled.

Charly eased the front door open with a hand on her hip and a sinister smile.

Lola raised her brows, pursed her lips, then walked in. Her shock of naturally bleached-looking blond curly hair was all over her head as usual, and her cinnamon skin, which Charly had never seen blemished, glowed more than normal, making her light blue eyes glow. "Hmm. You don't even have to tell me. Your look says it all. Let me guess. Brigette's in one of her I'm-laid-off-and-pissed-at-the-world moods again?" Lola asked, setting her designer leather messenger bag on top of Charly's antique thrift-store book bag. Lola was superstitious and would never set a purse, or anything resembling one, on the floor. She believed if she did so, she'd go broke.

"Charly! I. Said. Is. That. You?" Brigette yelled again.

Stormy's pretty face popped around the corner, where she faithfully studied in the dining area. She smiled at Lola and shook her head at Charly. "Awful. Just awful. I'll be so glad when she goes back to work. You better hurry, Charly. Hurry up so you can work on your math," she reminded, pushing up her glasses on the bridge of her nose, then disappearing.

Charly waved Lola on. "Come on. You can wait in my room until I see what she wants. Probably some soda," Charly said, calling pop soda like the New Yorkers she'd heard on television.

"Yes, you better hurry, Charly. I heard Mr. Miller's been on one lately. They said his wife left him for another man, and ever since then he's been flunking everybody." Lola pushed back her blond porcupine-looking hairdo, reached a hand into her pocket, then pulled it out, balled up in a fist. She extended it toward Charly. "Here."

Charly reached out her hand to take whatever it was Lola was giving. "What's this?"

Lola released a wad of bills onto Charly's palm. "Uncle Steely's staying with us for a while."

Charly nodded, clearly confused by Lola's statement. "Your uncle's staying with you. Oh . . . kay? I'm not following."

"Hurry up, Charly! And bring that greedy Lola with

you," Brigette hollered. "I know she's here. She always is, like she don't got a home. Heck, I should claim Lola on my taxes as much as she's here and eating up all the food I work so hard to buy!"

Charly gave Lola an apologetic look as they walked through the living room, passing the old-school thirty-two-inch television, and made their way to the steps. "Sorry. Now what were you saying about your uncle?"

Lola waved away Charly's apology. "Sorry for what? Don't be. I'm not. *You* buy all the food I eat!" Lola covered her mouth and laughed. "I don't take Brigette serious." Lola's smile faded. "Uncle Steely. Don't you remember him? He's the one that steals any and everything not bolted down, including people's identity." She shrugged. "So I can't keep your money for you anymore 'cause when he steals it—and he will steal it, trust me—I can't afford to replace three hundred dollars."

Charly nodded at Lola's reasoning, and wished she were old enough to go open a savings account on her own, without Brigette's signature. "Two hundred and eighty-six bucks," she said, counting the last of the dead presidents, then shoving the wad into her pants pocket. "I won't have the rest of the cash for the phone—or the hundred-dollar cable bill Brigette keeps ragging me about—until Friday because I had to pay the electric company. But, thanks for keeping it as long as you did, Lola. If Brigette knew . . ."

"Oh, I know. It'd be spent at the mall or deposited in her account," Lola finished Charly's statement. "That's only two days away. I sure hope it hurries up and comes, for your sake. You can't keep walking around talking on that old clunk of a phone. Not with everyone thinking you're the ish!" Lola laughed.

"Charly . . . I'ma count to ten, and if you're not up here . . ." Brigette threatened.

Charly just shook her head and quickened her pace. She didn't feel like dealing with Brigette today or any day, truth be told. Her mom was a trip, and because she'd had Charly when she was sixteen, Brigette seemed to forget that she was the parent. Instead of a daughter, Charly was more like Brigette's maid and personal handmaiden, or like a roommate who footed bills but had no say, *and* a live-in nanny for Stormy, which Charly didn't mind. As far as Charly was concerned, she and Stormy were better off without the lady who'd given birth to them. It was peaceful and loving when she wasn't around, and when she was home it was hell.

Brigette was a modern-day demon-licious witch, complete with cascading fake hair and too ample cleavage, courtesy of the G-cup over-the-shoulder-boulder-holder she wore and, Charly finally realized that, like her, her mother was also a liar. So maybe, just maybe, Charly had inherited the dishonest gene because there were many things wrong with Brigette's barrage of questions and statements. One, Stormy had walked in the door only a couple of minutes ahead of Charly. Two, if there was "only static" showing on the television, how were "some" of the stations coming in? Three, no one could "slip" into that contraption her mom had called a girdle. It wasn't really a girdle, it was some magic bodysuit sort of thingy that two or more people had to literally tuck Brigette's fat inside, then she'd have to sleep in it for a day or two to *look* ten pounds lighter and a couple of sizes smaller. Four, Brigette hadn't actually called Charly to her; she'd only said her name and asked if *that* was Charly. And five, Lola was right; Brigette didn't buy most of the food they ate. In fact, Brigette was laid off, so how could she be working so hard to buy food?

Charly raised one foot high, then rushed it toward the floor with all her might, stopping short of stomping it on the carpeted stair. She then lifted the other, repeating the pretend stomp over and over with alternate feet, making her way up to her mother's bedroom and wishing that she could bang hard enough to make the stairwell shake. But as much as she wanted to pound her soles on the floor, she couldn't. Brigette, besides being a semi-lazy half-caring mother, was also a bit mentally unstable. She'd earned a reputation in her teenage days that still followed her. Brigette wasn't to be messed with. She'd been known to drag a woman or two down the street, face against the pavement, had cut more than one of her boyfriends, and had even made a policeman cry. Charly inhaled. No, she wouldn't test her mother. She may not have been her biggest cheerleader, but she was no fool.

"Ma'am?" Charly repeated again, cracking open the door to her mother's bedroom and sticking only her face inside the room. Lola pushed her all the way inside, causing her to almost trip and collide with her mom's backside. "You called me?" Charly's question came out in a sputter as she caught her balance, barely missing running into her mother's huge rear end.

Brigette was bent over, her panty-covered butt and

dented thighs facing Charly and Lola. Her head was upside down between her legs, and her face was barely visible beyond her nose because her boobs were in the way. With perfectly drawn-on brows, she scratched the scalp of her lace-front wig with inch-long acrylic nails, making the expensive hair move side to side as if she'd grown it.

"Why you so nervous all the time, Charly?" she asked, her face peeking between the inverted V her thick legs were opened in. Unsuccessfully stretching her hands toward her feet, she seemed stuck, and had apparently been trying to lace up high heels that tied in a crisscross around her calves. The size of her gut prevented her from bending all the way to accomplish the task. There was just too much stomach to allow her full access to the laces. She let out a *whew*, unfolding herself to a stand. She stuck out a foot. "Tie this up for me. I don't know what's going on. For some reason, I'm a little winded today."

"Yeah, right. Too much weight," Lola muttered, lowering her tone with each word, and making Charly giggle.

Brigette snaked her neck. "What the . . . ? What did you just say, you lil' fast heffa?" she barked at Lola.

Lola smiled and shrugged her shoulders. "Nothing, Ms. Brigette. I only said it's not *right*. If you put on the shoes now, it'll be harder to put on the girdle. And . . . I wouldn't want anything to happen to those shoes. They're really nice."

"Yeah. Those are nice, Brigette," Charly enthusiastically agreed, not meaning a word of it. The shoes were atrocious, and looked like a pair of high-heeled Egyptian sandals that someone had once worn in Anytime B.C.

Brigette straightened until she looked taller, then squared her shoulders. She lowered her lids to a squint, and looked at Charly as if she was trying to figure out if she was being truthful or not. Her nose wiggled; then she scrunched it, raising her top lip toward her nostrils like something was stinking. Sucking her teeth, she put her hands on her hips, then stuck out her foot farther, twisting it side to side. She smiled. "Yeah. But they're more than nice. I paid almost two hundred for these." She snapped her fingers, then pointed to the magic bodysuit on the bed. "Get that bottom piece, Charly, and let's get this over with. I got a hot date, and I need to be breathing by the time he gets here. It's a new one with a panty and upper. It just came in the mail, so you know what that means. It's new so it'll take a couple hours just to inhale right."

Charly did as she was told, then squatted, stretching out one leg opening of the contraption as much as she could while her mother stepped in. Lola followed suit, grabbing the other side of the girdle. She nodded at Charly, indicating she was ready. With all of their strength, they stretched, tugged, pulled, and hiked the too-small girdle out and over and up Brigette's thick thighs and hips, then proceeded to work on part two. Wrapping the what'cha-ma-jig over her stomach and breasts, they tucked in the excess fat where they could and patted what they couldn't until it was flat as possible to help disguise the weight.

"And the fat is gone, baby. Gone! Yeah. Whew,"

Brigette sighed like she'd done some actual work to fit into the contraption that only disguised and reassigned her fat to different sections of her body, and not made it disappear like she believed. Holding her head high, she whirled to her full-length mirror, switching her walk to that of a runway model. She tossed her hair, did a full spin, then turned back sideways. She gave herself another once-over. "See this?" she asked, patting her now-flatter tummy. "Gone!" She moved her hands over her huge breasts, then trailed them down her middle, moving them to her back, and rounded them over her butt. "A work of art. Curves like these will make a blind man dizzy. I'm so chiseled even a man who can't see *can* see this Coca-Cola bottle shape!"

Charly crinkled her brows and looked at an equally confused-looking Lola. "All right. Can I go now, Brigette?"

Brigette froze. "Uhm. Let me see. . . ." She looked at Charly, deep thought registering across her forehead in wrinkles. She put her finger to her temple, contemplating. "Hell no! This house needs to be cleaned. My sheets need to be changed, and the toilet . . . when was the last time you gave my toilet a good hand wash?"

Lola shook her head. *Run, Charly! Run!* she mouthed, not uttering a sound.

Charly's phone did a jig in her pocket, then began chirping. With each sound it got louder and louder. "My job alarm," she explained to everyone, turning toward the door so she could run and change into her work uniform. "Brigette, I gotta get to work." Her words were apologetic. "Okay?"

Brigette laughed. "Okay? Okay? Heck, someone around

here has to punch a clock, and since I'm laid off, who better than you? You can clean up when you get home tonight. And you better learn how to hustle faster than you have been. How you gonna work at the plant with me making cars, if you don't? You know you ain't smart enough for college, so you might as well come with me. That is, if they call us back to work."

Lola grabbed Charly's arm on their way out of Brigette's bedroom. "Don't worry about your math, Charly. I had Mr. Miller last semester, and I know what it takes to get a high grade. I'll do your homework for you."

Charly wrapped Lola in a sisterly embrace. "I owe you one!" she said, then began hopping out of her pants on the way to her room. She threw them in the corner, then reached for a pair of tights. Her stomach growled. "And as long as I owe you . . ."

"Yeah. I know. I know. As long as you owe me I'll never go broke. I've heard that before, but I still only got lint in my pockets," Lola said, picking up Charly's shoes and handing them to her. "I'll meet you at your job later. I know my moms isn't cooking. And you know I gotta eat."

# 3

The heavy glass door pressed on the back of Charly's feet, helping to push her inside of Smax's BBQ. Charly, normally irritated by the weight of the door, was thankful for it today. She walked through the almost-empty restaurant, nodding her head at the few regulars. A crazy remix of Diana Ross, Stevie Wonder, and James Brown blared from grease-laden speakers wired to the stand in the corner where DJ the DJ spun real vinyl records. Immediately, she bopped her head. She was either an old soul trapped in a young body or she'd grown to like music from the sixties and seventies. "Hi, Rudy," she greeted Rudy-Rudy-Double-Duty, the self-nicknamed old head who was a double war vet, and had been patronizing Smax's since it opened its doors eons ago.

"Charly, Charly? Where ya been all my life? You know nobody can slice corn bread like you," Rudy teased.

"Yes, Charly, my dear. You're late, aren't you?" Dr.

Deveraux El asked, glancing down to his heirloom watch. Dr. Deveraux El was an older gentleman around fifty, and he had the name and debonair air of a man of nobility. When Brigette met him, she had called him a younger Billy Dee Williams, and Charly had agreed, though she had no idea who Billy Dee Williams was.

"No, sir, Dr. Deveraux El. I'm on time, as always. You know I'm in school. . . ."

Dr. El nodded, then held up a cup of tea, his pinky finger in the air. "Deveraux, Charly. Just call me Deveraux."

Charly smiled and nodded. They went through the same dance at least twice a week. She'd always address him as doctor and he'd always correct her. If only Dr. Deveraux El didn't have such a superior air, she could call him by his first name. "Okay, sir. I mean Deveraux."

The bottoms of her bowling shoes made kissing noises as Charly walked past the counter and into the kitchen's walk-in freezer to retrieve a ten-pound bag of fries, knowing her legs would freeze in the knee-length bebop skirt she'd found at a thrift store. "Yuck." Grease, flour, and God only knew what else was stuck to the brick-red commercial tile of the greasy spoon she slaved in for over twenty hours a week after school, but she wouldn't complain. She needed the job and liked the people.

"Charly, gal," Smax, the owner, greeted her when she shut the freezer door closed behind her.

Charly looked over toward the grill and grinned so hard her freshly blushed cheeks warmed. Smax was a sight for all eyes. Barely four-eleven, he wore his gray hair in long finger waves, and his thick mustache was curled up and over at the ends like a ram's horns. His mouth was literally glowing, with both his widely spaced front teeth, outlined by crowned gold with diamonds in the center. Today he wore electric-blue alligator shoes and a matching three-piece suit with a yellow shirt underneath. Charly's eyes moved to the coatrack in the rear, and, sure enough, an equally bright blue Dobbs hat hung there. Finger waves or no, Smax wouldn't be caught dead without a coordinating brim to match his outfit.

"Afternoon, Smax. I made it here on time. I just had to get some fries to drop."

Smax nodded, removing a custom-made gold toothpick from his mouth. He glanced at the clock, then Charly. "I know. I know. I keeps up with all my women." He winked.

Charly put a hand on her hip. "Smax, remember this isn't nineteen-seventy-nothing. You're out of the game, and you have no women on the street. Especially not me!" She laughed.

"And not me either!" Bathsheba, Smax's common-law wife, yelled from the small office that also served as the supply room. "Smax ain't never pimped nothing but food. Don't let them suits fool you, Charly!" she said, laughing a smoky, sultry laugh.

Smax nodded at Charly, winking twice. "Yessir, I ain't served nothing but food as far as Bathsheba and the po-pos are concerned." He walked toward Charly, bent slightly forward, and cupped his hands on either side of his mustache. He whispered, "Serving ribs and grilling meat cain't buy all this here, youngin'. Back in my day—"

"I can hear you, Smax," Bathsheba interrupted. "And

you ain't had no day. Don't listen to that old fool, Charly."

Smax nodded. "If you want the truth, you better listen. I got all the answers!" he said, then laughed, patting his knee before going back to tend the grill.

Charly joined him and Bathsheba in laughter, and wished they could adopt her. As odd as they looked to others on the outside, they were more than perfect within. Smax played the part of washed-up aged-out hustler, and Bathsheba knew her role, never carrying herself as anything less than a queen.

"C'mon back here, Charly, before you drop them fries," Bathsheba said.

Tucking the heavy cold bag under one arm, Charly winked at Smax, then went to the office. "Ma'am?" she said.

Bathsheba reached into her bra, then pulled out five twenty-dollar bills folded neatly into a handkerchief. "This here is your pay from last week. You didn't pick it up, remember? So you want it now, or you want me to keep holding it until you save for whatever you're saving for? 'Cause I know you're saving for something; that's the only time you lag on picking up your money."

Charly smiled, then extended her hand to take the money. "I'm ready for it now, Ms. Bathsheba. It took months, but by Friday I'll finally have enough for the phone."

"Phone?! *Phone?* You mean to tell me you've been slaving for a phone? Child, there's a rotary phone out there hanging on the wall you can use anytime. Besides, what kinda phone costs months' worth of paychecks?"

She held out the money like bait, obviously not intending to hand it over until Charly answered her question.

"A cell phone—"

"A cell—" Bathsheba interrupted.

"No. Yes. But not just *any* cell phone. This is *the* cell phone of all cell phones. I can go on the Internet like I would do now if I had a computer—"

"If? What you mean *if*? I thought you bought one 'round last Christmas. Wasn't that what you was saving for last time?" Bathsheba's brows drew together and her arms crossed over her breasts.

Charly nodded. "Yes, ma'am. But Brigette . . ." Bathsheba's forehead furrowed. She'd warned Charly that calling her mother by her first name wasn't going to be tolerated at Smax's. It was too disrespectful, despite Brigette's insistence. ". . . Sorry. My mom needed it for her car."

"Hmm. You mean your momma took it and gave it to Rudy-Rudy to install some overpriced radio in her car and put them ugly twenty-something-inch rims on her wheels. I know what be going on 'round here, even if I don't say nothing. Ain't that right, Smax?" she yelled out. "You know he's listening."

Charly's head moved up and down again. She had no defense for her mother's constantly "borrowing" Charly's hard-earned money and never paying it back.

"The phone will also help me study for school, take the online acting classes that I need, and I can video and video conference, even submit e-headshots and résumés to talent agencies. Remember my acting. . . . You and Smax have been to two of my plays."

"Four, not two." Bathsheba handed Charly her pay. She nodded. "We've been to all four of your plays. Besides your sister and that little blond-haired, blue-eyed, red-looking girl you run with—God only knows what kinda genes that girl got. What black girl is naturally blond and blue with red skin?—well, anyway, besides them, we were the only ones there."

Charly nodded. "Thank you."

Bathsheba gave Charly a once-over. "Don't thank me. It seems you're the closest I'll ever come to grandchillun at the rate my girls ain't producing. Now take that money and hide it, Charly. Hide it until you ready to pay for that phone. What you need to do is what I do. I keep telling you. Fold your money in a hanky and pin it to your bra. Can't nobody steal it that way without you knowing."

"I will, ma'am," Charly assured her, taking the money and stuffing it into her pocket. Then she walked out the office and pivoted toward the huge walk-in freezer. She needed to drop the fries for the early evening rush of customers.

"Charly?" Bathsheba called again.

Charly about-faced, then retraced the few steps she'd taken to leave the office. "Ma'am?" she said, popping her head back into the room.

Bathsheba raised perfectly arched brows, then shook her head and tsked. "Ya know it's a doggone shame the way your momma keep stealing your money. 'Cause that's what it is—thieving. Now get that money out your pocket and pin it to your brassiere."

\*   \*   \*

Charly zigzagged back and forth behind the front counter, refilling coffee cups and water glasses, then completed her usual maze to the small, square, dining tables situated around the dance floor. "All right," she urged on Betty and Louie, two heavy-eating regulars who visited from the nearby assisted-living facility so they could grub and mingle. They were doing their rendition of bebop, barely moving, and hooting their respective fraternity and sorority calls. Charly nodded, hoping she'd be as lively as they when she reached her seventy-fifth birthday.

She was bussing a table when she heard her name. Without turning, she knew it was Lola. Lola always came into Smax's like she owned the place, eating and drinking for free, and with good reason as far as Charly was concerned. Smax was rumored to be Lola's biological father, and if put side by side, no one could deny what Lola's mother and Smax so vehemently did. Lola was Smax's love child. Point blank. Period. Even Bathsheba, though she hated to admit it because she and Smax had been a couple longer than anyone could count, had to agree there must be some truth to the gossip. But like everyone else could deduce, some truth was like someone being a little bit pregnant—either it was or it wasn't. There was no halfway point. And Lola was Smax's.

"The usual?" Charly called out to Lola, her back still turned to her friend. "Half slab, coleslaw, two slices of white bread, and cobbler?"

"Charly! Charly!" Lola answered, her breath coming out in spurts.

Charly turned to face a frantic and approaching Lola. Immediately, she stiffened. She hadn't seen Lola so distraught since she'd discovered that Smax—"the old pimp with a limp," as she'd called him—was her daddy. "What's wrong? You okay?"

Lola grabbed her by the arm, snatched the towel out of her hand, and threw it on the table. "We gotta go. Now!"

Charly snatched away. "You know I gotta work. What is it?"

Lola put a hand on each of Charly's cheeks. "Look at me. We. Gotta. Go. Now. I just ran into Mason, and he's coming here. After he drops off his new dog to the pet salon so you can help groom it. Did you tell him you worked there?"

Charly shook her head. He must not have heard her clearly. She'd said she'd applied, not that she worked there. Her jaw fell. Lola was right. She had to leave immediately. "Smax isn't going to let me leave. You know that. Can you ask him?"

Lola shook her head. "Nope. He said I can't get nothing from him but free food, which you know is a dead giveaway that he's my pops because he doesn't give away a plate. He said if I asked for one more thing, the food'll stop. I guess I'm supposed to eat all the back child support he'd owe if my mom grew a spine, 'fessed up to the affair, and took him to court. I love you, Charly. Love you like a sister, but I can't and won't give up my free meals for you."

Charly nodded. She'd gone hungry many nights because her mom was just as lowdown as Lola's. "Okay." She picked up the towel, threw it over her shoulder, then excused herself. If Lola couldn't ask him to let her off early, she would have to do it herself. But how? She put her hands on her hips while she thought.

"I got an idea," Lola offered. "It's so not the truth, but it'll get you off." Lola walked over to her, then whispered her saving grace in Charly's ear.

Pushing open the half door that led to the kitchen, Charly looked left and right to see if Bathsheba was anywhere in sight. She exhaled. She didn't see the first lady of Smax's anywhere near the grill. Relief moved through her. What she was about to do was going to go straight over Smax's finger-waved head, but Bathsheba was sharp, and Charly knew she wouldn't go for it.

"Smax. Smax," Charly barely whispered, waving the towel in the air.

"What?" he answered her distress call, his whisper even lower than hers.

Charly pointed toward the walk-in freezer, where she speed-walked, waving him on to follow her in case he didn't get the message.

"Dang, Charly! It's doggone cold in here. What is it?" he asked, shifting his feet in place to keep warm as if he'd been in the freezer for hours, not seconds.

"I gotta go, Smax. Now. It's an emergency."

Smax shook his head. "I need you—"

"Lola's mother's brother, Steely, is in town, and he's trying to come up here to get some free food he says you owe him. You know he's a thief, and he's hinted at you being Lola's . . . you know. Lola thinks he may be coming to clown, so I assured her—over the speaker phone so he could hear the conversation—that I was getting off early and would bring him some ribs."

Smax just stood there, nodding. "You all right, you know that, don't ya, Charly? Go 'head. Take two full slabs of ribs, and don't worry about your check. I'll pay you for the full day."

*Yes!* Charly praised her newest lie. She felt kind of sorry for lying to Smax, but she had to get to the pet salon, and talk her way into a part-time job there. She knew it probably wouldn't happen, but she didn't want to let Mason down.

# 4

Charly bolted down the street with the wind against her face, but nothing blocked her determination. She had to get a position in the shop, even if they only allowed her to sweep the floor. Turning the corner at full speed, she hoped there was only some lowly employee working there, one who wouldn't care one way or another. That's what she needed because she had no pet experience to speak of, so being qualified for the job was out of the question. A car horn blared when she ran into the intersection, forgetting to look both ways. She'd become so focused on her destination that safety hadn't crossed her mind. Over her shoulder, she could see Lola moving slower than a slug, taking her time following. Lola was clearly in no rush. *But*, Charly thought, *why would she be?* Lola wasn't the one who'd lied and was trying to avoid eating her words.

"Here. Here. Here!" Charly said, skidding to a stop.

She'd run so fast that she'd just passed the salon, and had to backtrack. Fixing her hair and wiping off perspiration from her face, Charly looked over her outfit, adjusting it where necessary. Squaring her shoulders, she stood tall, then opened the door and entered.

"We'll be with you in a second," a young girl not much older than Charly said, then disappeared through a doorway behind the counter.

"We" jumped out at Charly and made her pulse race. She'd been hoping to find one person at the salon, believing it would've made her chances of bargaining herself into working some measly chore. That's all she needed to make it look as if she were employed there when Mason showed. Something simple.

"Okay," Charly said, drumming her fingers on the counter, then walking around the waiting area, scouting the place. A pampered pet pamphlet caught her eye, and she picked it up. The salon offered a lot to pets and their owners. Way more than she would've guessed. Who knew that puppies had pedicures and facials and Pooch Smooch mouthwash for "kissers"? *Yuck*. Sucking face with a dog was totally disgusting and ridiculous.

"How can I help you?" a cheery younger woman asked. She wore a white lab coat, and looked more like a veterinarian than a pet groomer.

"See you tomorrow." The first girl Charly had seen walked out from the back, waving. "Hopefully my fever will break by then."

"Feel better," the veterinarian-looking pet groomer said.

Charly pasted a smile on her face. "Actually, I was

coming here to ask you the same thing. How can I help you?"

The woman smiled. "I'm sorry. Does that mean you're looking for a job? Because if so, I can take your application, but, we've hired someone already so, at the moment, we're not—"

The door opened and an old-fashioned bell, situated where the door would barely hit it, rang, cutting off the woman. A German shepherd walked in, leashed to a young lady who had her cell pressed to her ear. The lady announced herself and her dog without ever ending her phone conversation, signed a sign-in sheet, then took a seat.

"One moment," the shop worker said, typing something into the computer.

The woman nodded, still babbling into the phone while trying to make the German shepherd sit.

The bell dinged again and the door opened. This time an older woman carrying a pet carrier came in. "I'm afraid Orion needs an emergency cleaning. He regurgitated and got it all over himself. Isn't that right, Orion?" she said into the opening of the carrier.

The lady behind the counter kept her cool, but Charly could tell that she was pressed. German shepherd and Cell Phone Lady obviously had an appointment, but the lady with Orion didn't. Charly took the cue as the opportunity she'd been waiting for, then leaned against the counter and read the lady's name tag. "Rebecca, you sure I can't help you? You seem to be alone."

Rebecca did one of the things Charly knew she would,

and would've bet they had taught it to Rebecca in pet salon school. She smiled. "We don't have any openings—"

"Are you sure? What if the sick girl doesn't come back?" Charly pressed.

The bell ding-a-linged again, and in walked a gentleman dressed in an obviously expensive high-end suit, cradling underneath his arm the ugliest mushed-faced dog Charly had ever seen. "Barkly's here early for his pre-paid standing appointment. We're ahead of schedule today, and would like to stay that way. You understand and will accommodate, right?" he announced, making his way to the counter.

Charly scooted to the side to allow him room to sign in seconds before the bell rang again. Lola smiled and waved.

Rebecca exhaled loud and long, and her cheeks flushed. Overwhelmed wasn't the word for the look that blanketed her face. She stared at the computer monitor, clearly looking at the bookings. Charly stood taller on tiptoe, and saw that the salon was only booked for one appointment before Mason's, and none of the pets or owners occupying the waiting room were it, not even the shepherd.

"Yes?" Rebecca asked Lola with raised what-do-you-want brows, shirking her usual "How can I help you?"

Lola made her way next to Charly, and Charly nudged her in the ribs. "Oh, you're the girl with two show cats, right?" Charly asked her, not really knowing the difference between a house cat and a show cat, but remembered some animal show on television making a big to-do about show cats and competitions.

Lola gave her the side eye; then Charly nudged her again. Lola nodded, finally getting the hint. "Yes," she said. "Three, actually."

Rebecca's eyes widened, and Charly couldn't tell if it was because she was excited at the possibility of grooming show cats or because she was overwhelmed.

"And we have a competition coming up, and my groomer is ill," Lola said, making the lie even more believable. "Can we bring them in in like an hour? You and this salon will get credit, of course. So is that a yes?" she asked Rebecca.

Rebecca nodded and her eyes glossed over. She was on the verge of crying, and Charly knew it. Courtesy of Brigette, she'd been there too many times before not to recognize being worked like a slave. She curled her finger in a come-here fashion, then whispered to Charly, "I can't lose my job. I can't. And if I lose one more client, that's it. And this is the only way I can pay for school."

"I told you I got you, Rebecca. You don't even have to worry about paying me." Charly went around the counter, found her way to the back office, and grabbed a lab jacket. She slipped it on, scrunching up the too short sleeves to make it look like her own. "Barkly! We're ready for you," she called out, returning to the front, opting for the smaller pooch without vomit on his coat. She didn't do throw-up or big dogs, so Barkly was easiest. "I'll personally take care of him," she told his owner.

Barkly was washed and the German shepherd was getting a pedicure before Charly knew it. She'd gone into nanny mode and found washing dogs easier than she'd thought, once she'd figured out how to use the sprayer, and cleaned up the sudsy catastrophic mess she'd created. When she was allowed to put a gentle muzzle around the dogs' mouths to prevent them from nipping, it became even simpler. To her surprise, they were all gentle and loving, even the big dog who could've taken her down with one snap.

"You're not so bad, Charly," Rebecca said, tying a red hankie around the German shepherd's neck. "I don't know why you showed up here, or where the girl with the three show cats went, but I'm glad you did." She shrugged. "I wish I could say the owner's hiring, but she's not. We could really use someone around here like you, especially because you helped save my job. A job I can't afford to lose."

Charly shrugged her shoulders, too. "Don't worry. You already paid me by letting me help out. Plus, I already have a job, Rebecca."

The front bell rang again, and Charly's heart dropped. Without looking, she knew it was Mason. Had to be.

"One second," Rebecca called out. She wiped her hands on her lab coat, then patted the shepherd's head. "So why are you here, Charly? Really?" she asked, heading toward the front of the salon.

Charly pointed toward the waiting area. "Him. There's this guy I like who thinks I work here . . . a dumb lie I told. Don't ask me why. Anyway, please just let me do this. He just got a dog and was bringing it here because I—"

"Work here? I got'cha. I did stupid stuff too when I was your age," Rebecca said, then laughed for the first time since Charly had been there. "Well, c'mon. Favor granted. He's yours then."

Charly followed Rebecca to the front and almost froze. Mason stood on the other side of the counter with the cutest ugly-faced dog she'd ever seen. Well, it wasn't really a cute dog, but to her it was because it belonged to Mason.

"Charly," he said. "I wasn't sure if you were here today. Anyway, meet Brooklyn, my bulldog puppy."

Charly, totally forgetting that she hated dogs, made her way around the counter and relieved Mason of Brooklyn. Cuddling the puppy like a baby while Mason explained to Rebecca what Brooklyn needed, Charly oohed and ahhed, telling the dog that she was going to take care of her. Mason went and sat. Rebecca laughed, loud and clear, snagging Charly's attention.

Charly crinkled her eyebrows together. "What's so funny?" she asked, taking the dog around the back of the counter.

"You're taking care of her, all right. You said you wanted her, and you asked for the favor, so you got it."

Charly shrugged. "Okay, thanks! So? How bad can it be?"

Rebecca bit her lip, then made a face. "Depends on how badly she's impacted."

"Impacted . . . ?" Charly repeated. "And that means?"

"Brooklyn needs to be expressed."

Mason made his way back to the counter. "Since I know you have my back, Charly, I know Brooklyn's okay with you. No offense, miss," he said, turning to Rebecca. Then he locked eyes with Charly. "I hate to leave, but my moms needs me. I know you got this. Right, baby?" he asked, nodding his head toward his dog. "You'll call me when she's ready, right? Or do you want to bring her to me? I like option two, myself."

Charly nodded. "No problem. I'll bring her to your house. You know I got'chu, Mason!" she said, enthusiastically, then whispered to Rebecca, "What's that? Expressed?"

"I hope you really like him! You need to squeeze all the poopy stuff out of the dog's anal glands. Maybe even finger scoop it out. But that's not the only one, Barkly too. You told his owner you'd take care of him. His bath wasn't a real bath, just a prewash before the expression. No worries, though. I'll help with his so you'll know how with Brooklyn."

# 5

Her fingers were going to fall off. Petrify into rock, then shatter and scatter to the ground in miniscule granules. That's what she believed and, in a way, that's what she wanted. Squeezing a dog's anal glands had not been a part of her Hooking Mason by Any Means Necessary plan, and the way Brooklyn's butt smelled, she knew her nostrils were in trouble. And she hadn't even started the expression.

"The gland openings should be somewhere around the five-o'clock and seven-o'clock positions of the openings. Remember?" Rebecca asked.

Charly grimaced. She'd been face to dog's butt for too long, and was ready to run. But she couldn't. Putting her right hand under Brooklyn's stomach, she adjusted her until Brooklyn's rectum was directly in front of her. With her thumb and forefinger, she pressed gently but firmly against the skin under the anal gland openings, feeling for something about the size of a kidney bean. "Yuck!" she said, feeling the odd shape that was more enlarged than Barkly's had been.

"You got it," Rebecca said. "Now press and squeeze at the same time. Think of popping a pimple. You press and squeeze around the perimeter, pushing up at the same time."

Charly gagged. She pressed her forefinger on one side and her thumb on the other of the inflamed bump, then squeezed, moving her digits in an upward motion.

"Towel. Towel. Towel!" Rebecca yelled, reminding Charly.

Greenish-brown gooey secretions squirted from Brooklyn's bottom, making Charly jump back and to the right. Her face contorted, and she squealed like a pig. She was afraid to look down, scared that some of the mess had gotten on her. Yes, she wanted to please her boyfriend, well, *almost* boyfriend, but even she had to question if she wanted to be liked so badly that she'd wear his dog's mess.

"You're good," Rebecca said, laughing. "It didn't get you." She reached over and handed Charly a warm towel. "Now cover it this time."

Charly happily accepted the towel and placed it over Brooklyn's anus. Still gagging from the smell, sight, and thought of what she was doing, she expressed and expressed and expressed until Brooklyn had no more greenish-brown anal secretions.

Rebecca clapped like she was at a concert. "I'm proud of you. Now you can bathe her."

\*    \*    \*

Charly held up her hand to the waning sun in front of the salon. Her fingers had been to a place they shouldn't have gone, and done things they shouldn't have done. She looked down at Brooklyn, glad that she had been the second victim. That's how Charly thought of the dogs she and Rebecca had freed from their built-up anal secretions—violated. There was no way anyone—man or animal—could go through something like that and not feel victimized by an injustice.

Brooklyn whimpered, sitting on her bottom, refusing to move. Charly felt bad for her, knowing it had to be sore. Getting all that gunk out of the dog had not been easy, and the whole "expressing" had given her new appreciation for being human. "Come on, Brooklyn," she gently urged, tugging lightly on the leash.

Brooklyn wouldn't move. In fact, it seemed as if she was getting heavier by the second. Charly put her free hand on her hip. "Brooklyn, we can't do this. I know you don't want to stay here all day. Do you?"

Brooklyn whined.

Charly crouched down, getting as close to eye level as she could with the small dog as passersby moved to and fro, looking at Charly and the dog taking up the middle of the busy sidewalk. "Okay, let's make a deal. You walk, and I promise to get you some treats. At the rate we're moving, we're going to get run over. And I can't have that." She stood and pulled on the leash again. No luck.

"She's not ready," a voice called from behind, stealing her attention from Brooklyn. It was the distinguished gentleman who'd brought Barkly into the salon, and by his side was Barkly. "She's a pup, and it seems as if she hasn't been trained to walk yet."

*Walk yet?* What dog needed to be taught to walk? Charly wondered, smiling at the man as if she was well aware of the problem. "I know, but I always like to give them a chance to prove me wrong. Sometimes I think they're smarter than us. Take Barkly, for example. He's such a pro, he almost groomed himself."

The man smiled and froze mid-move. He'd been reaching toward his breast pocket. "Don't speak so soon, you might smite yourself."

*Smite?* "How so?" Charly asked, standing.

The man stuck his hand inside his suit, then pulled out a wallet. Unfolding it, he opened it lengthways, then fished out two twenty-dollar bills. "Your tip. You don't want to smite—cut yourself off—from getting the tip you earned. I forgot to leave it."

Charly accepted the money with a thankful grin. "Wow! Thank you. But isn't this too much? This has to be more than the groom cost."

He shook his head. "No. No need to thank me. My Barkly's never been so clean or smelled so good. And money is not an option when it comes to my baby," he said with a polite nod. He turned and began to walk away, pulling on Barkly's leash. "One more thing." He looked back over his shoulder. "Next week, then?"

Charly's eyebrows rose. She didn't know what he meant by "next week," but she knew why Barkly was so clean and fresh. After he'd been expressed, she'd washed him for almost an hour straight because she'd spilled so much concentrated shampoo on him, then took forever to rinse him. He was her first lesson on too much soap, and had been the first initiated into what she and Rebecca called Charly's Doubly Bubbly Club.

"Yes. Barkly and I will see you next week. If you're not available, we'll have to look elsewhere for a groomer. After today, I know he wasn't shampooed properly before you came. Isn't that right, Barkly?" he asked his dog as if Barkly could speak.

Charly nodded. On one hand, the man was paying her a compliment, but on the other side of his decision, he was ousting Rebecca out of a job. Rebecca had told her she couldn't lose one more client, which Charly took to mean she'd had to have lost some before. Charly nodded. She'd have to fix that. Rebecca had looked out for her, so she owed her. She wouldn't let her shampooing skills get in the way of Rebecca and college, even if she, herself, wasn't a big fan of textbooks.

Charly took the forty dollars and stuffed the bills deep into her skirt pocket. In only a few hours at the pet salon, she'd made more than she would've at Smax's, and it sure felt good. Not wonderful enough to make her want to turn her back on the retirees who patronized the restaurant, because she'd grown to love all the regulars and her bosses, but still, it was nice. Mentally, she calculated how much she'd saved. There was the two-hundred-eighty-six that Lola had returned, and now forty. "Three-hundred and twenty-six," she said, proudly. With the money Bathsheba had given her and her upcoming paycheck on Friday, she'd have enough money for the phone (which she had to buy outright because she was too young to enter a contract), a jazzy case, and maybe even the first month's service. "C'mon Brooky-Brook," she said to Brooklyn, scooping her from the ground. "We don't want to keep Mason waiting," she said, then prepared to help Brooklyn walk the half mile to Mason's house.

Before Charly could ring the doorbell, Mason opened the door, barely clothed. Charly gulped, taking in his boxer shorts and extra-white wifebeater undershirt. The sight of him, minus his usual outfit of jeans, sneakers and latest hottest shirt, knocked the wind out of her. She stammered, almost unable to contain herself, but she did. Swallowing her feelings, she calmed herself. She wouldn't let him know he had her. "Here's Brooklyn," she said, still on the porch, not wanting to appear pushy by just inviting herself in. Reluctant, and a bit saddened, she handed over the dog. It amazed her how she'd gone from being uncomfortable around four-legged creatures to actually knowing she was going to miss Brooklyn. In the short time they'd spent together, she'd grown kind of fond of the puppy who'd shot fecal waste from her anus, then held Charly with sweet innocent eyes, almost as if she was trying to thank her.

Mason took Brooklyn and rubbed her head. "Come in, Charly," he said, opening the door wider and standing to the side, allowing her room to enter. "How much do I owe you?"

Charly just stood there, not knowing what to do. She shrugged. "Don't worry about it. Look at it as my apology for being late on helping you write your paper."

A weird look moved across Mason's face. "Well, about that . . . I think I may be okay." He ran his hands over Brooklyn's head again, then looked at Charly's feet. His whole demeanor screamed foul play.

Charly reared back her head. It was only recently that Mason had been so pressed about the English paper, so his dismissing it had taken her aback. "Really?" She raked her fingers through her hair in aggravation.

"Mason?" a girl's voice called from another room.

Mason's head shot up, and his look moved from weird to guilty. "Well, I kinda had help from a friend," he said apologetically.

Charly's eyebrows rose and strands of hair fell in her face. "*Friend?*" She was Mason's only friend, at least that's what she'd believed. "Really?" she asked again, a bit of attitude flaring. "I didn't know you had a *friend*," she said, swiping hair from her eyes. Something was in one, irritating it, and it was starting to water. Blinking deliberately and slowly, she was thankful for the interruption because it gave her time to check herself. Jealousy was starting to surface, and that was unacceptable. So what if another girl had helped him with his stupid paper? So what if the same girl was there and calling his name when it should have been her? She tried to convince herself that it didn't matter. After all, she told herself, she wasn't his *girlfriend* girlfriend. Yes, they were together in theory, but he hadn't actually asked her to be his girl. Then she wondered if guys still asked girls to be exclusive.

"Well, that's good, Mason." She forced a smile. "I'm

glad you got it done." Her feet shuffled anxiously, and her lids batted away the tears forming in the stinging eye. She was ready to go.

A relieved look washed his face of the guilty mask he'd worn. "I'm glad you're being such a good sport about it. I know I pressed you about it earlier."

"Mason?" the voice called again.

Charly shrugged her shoulders. "I probably should be going. I got a lot to do, ya know? And you might want to answer her."

Mason shook his head, then stepped outside and closed the door behind him. "No. I don't."

Her head spun left to the closed door, then right toward Mason. "You don't what?"

Mason did that thing he did with his brows again. Instantaneously, Charly's attitude began to melt. "No, I don't know what you gotta do, and I don't *have* to answer anyone." He put down Brooklyn, stepped forward, and grabbed Charly's face in his hands. "Stay still," he directed, moving her hair from her face, and stretching her eye with his thumb and forefinger. "Stay still. I almost got it," he said, grabbing the strand of hair that was poking her eye, then blew gently.

Charly backed away, an emotional mess. On one hand, his being so close made her want to get on tiptoe and kiss him; on the other, she wanted to punch him. He didn't need another girl to help him with anything. She was all he needed.

"I gotta go," she said, opening the door. "Before I have to get a *friend* to help me catch up with my work." She was down the steps, and speeding away from his house angrily. As much as she hated living in a small town, it had its benefits. Before the sun rose, Charly was sure she'd know two critical things: who Mason's friend was—and how to get rid of her.

# 6

Charly's dirty clothes were bunched up in the corner of her room, peeving her. She'd been so busy working, crunching homework assignments, stockpiling for the phone, and juggling her other chores—including Brigette's demands and looking after Stormy—that she'd neglected her own needs. Her laundry had piled, her acting practice had been abandoned, and, now, she had to figure out who was this friend of Mason's, pick up her check, finally get her cell and sign up for the online acting classes. She put her hands on her hips, surveying the area. It was a disaster. A bona fide, certified hot mess of a mess, and she couldn't leave it this way. She nodded, picking up a couple of loose socks. The first thing she had to do was clean her space; then she'd find a sixties costume to wear to Smax's while trying to get in touch with Rebecca from the pet salon so she could help save Rebecca's job before she lost it due to Barkly's owner insisting that she be Barkly's groomer.

Sorting the clothes, she remembered the money she'd put in the pockets of the pants and skirt she'd worn the other day. She couldn't forget that. Brigette had been known to search her and Stormy's pockets, taking whatever she found. Retrieving her savings, she scanned the room, looking for a hiding place. She didn't want to walk with so much money on her, afraid of losing it, a thing she'd done a time or two or three before. Her eyes roamed past the dresser, the makeshift nightstand she'd made out of old acting books, and the mattress. All three were too predictable, as was the worn carpet she'd pulled up to hide cash before, only to come back and find that Brigette had beat her to it. Charly snapped her fingers. "The closet." In the upper section, they'd stored old suitcases and boxes that were filled with Charly's old movie scene sketches, pictures of her dad, and lists of goals she was still determined to accomplish.

Grabbing a folding chair from next to the dresser, Charly dragged it across the room to the closet, then stepped up on it. On tiptoe, she managed to free one of the middle suitcases from the others. It was as big as it was heavy. It was also plain and dirty beige, something she was sure Brigette would overlook. She moaned under the weight of it, barely able to lower it from over her head without dropping it. "Don't slip. Don't slip," she begged the old beat-up baggage. If Brigette heard it thump on the floor, she'd come snooping. With suitcase in hand and feet firmly on the floor, Charly struggled to the bed, dropping it on the mattress and opening it. Sure enough, a big picture of her and her dad met her eyes and caused her to smile. She didn't know why seeing him made her happy. He'd left her years ago, but the best memories of her life involved him.

A soft knock at the door made her pause and tense. Then she relaxed. Brigette was too lazy to walk to the room unless she was looking for something, and then would only do so if no one was there. "One sec," Charly said, shuffling through pictures and papers, locating a place she could stash the money. In the corner of the suitcase, under a stack of rubber-band-wrapped index cards, she saw the lining of the case was torn. She nodded, folded the money as neatly and flatly as she could, then stuck it inside, pressing it until it seemed to meld with the case. She placed the homemade cue cards back over the slit, then covered it with the rest of the other contents. "I'm coming," she said, closing and lugging the case back over to the closet, where she shuffled two lighter ones to the side, then sandwiched the dusty beige one between them.

"Charly? Can I come in or not?" Stormy asked.

Charly closed the closet, picked up the folding chair, then put it back next to the dresser. "Yes," she said, out of breath, collapsing on top of the bed.

Stormy opened the door, then looked suspiciously around the room. "What are you up to?" she asked, then zoomed in on the pile of clothes. "Yuck! What happened in here?"

Charly shook her head. "This is not my bedroom; it's just where I dress and sleep. You know I'm too busy to clean up. Now I gotta get ready to go to Smax's." She got up, then rifled through drawers. "Foxy," she said, pulling out a glittery shirt. "Today, I'll dress up like Foxy Brown. Smax and Bathsheba will get a kick out of it. Now where's my wig?" she asked no one.

"Come on. I'll help you find it. I think it's great that you get to dress up for work," Stormy said, adjusting her glasses on her face before they slipped down her nose.

Charly looked at her sister. The glasses needed to be adjusted, and everyone knew it, but Brigette didn't care. "I know. It's really cool wearing different costumes. Plus, I don't like to go in looking like a waitress. How boring is that, and anyway dressing up helps me with my acting, Stormy. I use work to polish characters while getting paid." She held her index finger to her lips. "And today's payday, so you know I'm getting my phone when I get off," she whispered. "I'm so excited."

An afro wig was on her head, a wing-tip-collared button-up shirt was tied around her waist, and a pair of skintight bell-bottoms fit her like a second skin. Charly smiled, admiring herself in the reflection of the pet salon window. She looked like a younger version of the real Foxy Brown, except for her beloved chocolate combat boots with red laces. *Take that, Pam Grier*, she mouthed to her mirror image, then blew herself a kiss. A hand, waving from the other side of the glass, interrupted her. Charly clenched her teeth, a bit embarrassed at first, then shook it off. She was Ms. Too Everything to hold an ounce of embarrassment—too popular, too cute, and most importantly, too original. She was Charly St. James, star on the rise. She patted her afro until it was perfect, puckered her lips to smooth out her gloss, then smiled at Rebecca.

"Wow! Look at you," Rebecca said when Charly walked in. "Are you like an actress or something? The other day, you looked like one of the Supremes."

Charly smiled. "Yes, I'm an actress. And I didn't look like one of the Supremes. I was *the* top-billing Supreme. Diana Ross." She batted her drugstore-bought long fake lashes. "Is the owner here? I need to talk to you. We have a problem here at the salon."

Rebecca's brows raised in curiosity. "No. It's just me again. The owner's never here. The other girl is still sick, and the others only come in early mornings and on weekends. What problem do *we* have, Charly? You don't even work here." She laughed.

Charly's smile disappeared and her arms crossed. "Well, it seems I do. Or at least we're going to have to make it look like I do. I ran into Barkly's owner the other day after I"—she cringed—"expressed Barkly." She gave Rebecca the rest of the details.

Rebecca nodded, biting her bottom lip. "Okay. Okay. Okay," she said, clearly not knowing what to do. "I can't lose my job, Charly. Financial aid partially covers my tuition, and I use the money here to cover the rest, plus rent, food—"

"Yada, yada, yada. You need the money for life—to live. I know what you mean," Charly said, then walked behind the counter, and pulled up Barkly's standing appointment account. She drummed her fingers on the counter. "Okay, I got it. Barkly usually comes in when I'm working after school at the restaurant. . . ."

"Okay, that doesn't help," Rebecca said, sighing.

Charly slapped her hand on the counter. "It's cool. As long as it's just a shampoo, we're good. I can work it so I'm taking my break then, but you'll have to do the work. I'll just be here to greet the owner, check Barkly in, and take him to the back. They don't have to know who's grooming him. Get it?"

Rebecca chewed her bottom lip again; then she nodded. "But what if I have a lot of work? What if I can't do it? What if the other girl who works here doesn't go for it?"

Charly tried to scratch her scalp, but the wig was in the way. She hadn't considered all those things. She moaned in thought, snatched off the wig, then paced, raking her fingers through her hair. She stopped in front of a mirror, putting the fake hair back on, and watched herself transform from Charly to Foxy. The change made her light up. "I got it! Just like I looked like Diana Ross the other day with hair and makeup and really big sunglasses, my sister, Stormy, can do the same."

Rebecca's head almost spun off. "What?"

"My sister will come in on those days, costumed down. I mean, who can recognize me without my costumes? Not you and not Barkly's owner. I'll just send Stormy in in a different costume, and if there's a question, all she has to do is blame it on the costumes."

Rebecca nodded. "That may work, Charly. Because, the truth is, I don't know what you look like, you know, regular."

"But you'll have to pay Stormy and, maybe, give the other girl some hush money."

Rebecca smiled. "I can do that, no problem. If it means that I can finish school, I can do it."

Smax's roof was on fire. At least that's what all the old heads were chanting when Charly walked through the door, nodding her head to DJ's George Clinton/Parliament seventies remix that he was spinning so well. "Hey!" she said, bopping her way to the back to collect her pay.

"The roof. The roof is on fire!" the dancing crowd sang in unison.

"A late good evening to you, Charly," Dr. Deveraux El greeted her when she passed.

"Good evening to you too, Doc," Charly said. Today, she didn't have time to do the usual back and forth about how she should refer to him. Today she was here to do her job and get paid for it. She had things to do and people to see. Namely, the cell phone company.

"Hey, Mr. Rudy-Rudy," she said to the double war vet as she passed the end of the counter, deciding to get both of her favorite customers out of the way. The faster she got through them, the faster she could go see Bathsheba and collect her funds.

"Charly, you certainly are foxy today. Pun intended," Rudy said, patting his own afro. "I'm telling you, you're giving me flashbacks. And I'm not talking about the war either. That Pam Grier . . ." He shook his head, then drifted off to another time. "Whew—wee! I was something back then. *The*. Man."

\* \* \*

Charly pushed a chair up to the table, then straightened the flimsy white tablecloth. She moved the condiments to the middle, then looked to her left. Lola was standing there with a hand on her hip, a rib in another. "I'm coming. I'm coming," she said, not understanding why Lola was in such a rush. She was getting the phone, not Lola, but the way Lola was being impatient one would've thought it was her buying the hottest gadget.

"Ugh," she said, reaching in her shirt and scratching where she itched. The pay she'd just picked up was pinned to the inside of her shirt, thanks to Bathsheba and her handkerchiefing. Ever since the last time she'd lost her money, Bathsheba had tried to make her keep it in her "daily bank," aka her bra, and when Charly had refused, Bathsheba made her pin it to the inside of her shirt in a neatly folded handkerchief that was secured in a rubber band. The place was almost empty save for Rudy-Rudy, and Dr. Deveraux El, who had a spread of literature on aboriginal peoples' literature before him on the counter, and occasionally ranted about only his American people being nationless.

Lola smacked her lips and closed her eyes in pure euphoria. "Smax know he wrong for making sauce this good," she said, licking her fingers. "And what's Doc up to now? Who's nationless? I'm from America, and the last time I looked at the map, America was a nation."

Doc got up from his seat, and made his way over to Lola and Charly. In his hands, he had a stack of papers and a dictionary. "America, my dear sister, is *not* a nation, it's a country. And even that is debatable. Though used interchangeably, there is quite a diffence between the two. A country—America—is a self-governed political body. A nation is a tightly woven group of people who share a common culture." He nodded, then turned to Rudy-Rudy. "Isn't that correct, sir?"

Rudy agreed. "And I should know. I fought for the corporation."

"*The* corporation," Dr. Deveraux El parroted. "Indeed."

Lola twisted her face, looking from one older man to the next; then she turned to Charly, who shrugged. "Corporation? I thought you just said America is a country."

Smax came from the back with an orange towel thrown over his shoulder. Charly smiled. Only Smax could pull off the bright colors he donned himself in, and today his three-piece suit was burnt orange with matching alligator shoes and argyle socks that show every time he pulled up his too-long pants, which was often. "They ain't teaching y'all nothing in school! America is a country. The United States of America—where you think you live—is a corporation. Doodle it, and see."

Charly laughed. "You mean Google it, Smax."

Smax grabbed the towel off one shoulder, then slung it to the next. "Doodle it, Google it, smoodle it! It is what it T.I. is. Come on, Rudy and Doc, we're closing. Doc, we'll see you tomorrow, and, Rudy, we'll drop you off. Charly, you and this little greedy gal good? Or y'all need a ride too?"

"All I need is some of these to go," Lola said, holding up her bare rib bone.

Charly took off the apron she wore to bus tables, then folded it over and over. It was closing time, and she wasn't going to waste a second longer than she had to. The moment of her dreams had come, and the cellular store was waiting. It only stayed open an hour longer than Smax's, so she needed to hurry. "I'm good, Smax," she said, then tossed the towel to him. "You mind putting that up for me? I'm in a rush."

Smax caught the apron, then reminded her that she worked for him and not the other way around, then finished with, "Okay, Charly, but only this once." He turned to Lola. "And the only 'some of these' you getting, if you don't carry your greedy butt out of here, is these kicking you right in your bee-hind." He pointed to his wing-tipped orange shoes.

Lola sucked her teeth, then grabbed Charly by the arm. Suddenly, she stopped, then pointed at a television set. "Look at this, Charly. They're holding auditions for a new television show in New York next week. Too bad you won't be there."

The television died thanks to Smax's clicking the remote. "Y'all better go so I can lock up," he said.

"Let's go," Lola said to Charly, then mumbled under her breath to Smax, "That's why your short behind needs a stepstool to pee."

Charly handed Lola one suitcase, then another, as Lola set them down on the floor. Finally, the beige one was in her hands, and she could feel excitement shoot through her veins. In less than an hour, she'd have her phone and connection to the world via the Internet feature, the video camera, and all the apps it had.

"Pass it, Charly," Lola urged, hands held out, ready to

accept the weight of it, which Charly had warned her about.

Charly handed the heavy case to her best friend, then stepped off the chair and made her way to the bed. "Yayer!" she celebrated, dancing in a circle. With the addition of the hundred bucks she had pinned inside her shirt, she had all the money she needed to get the phone, plus cash to pay the bills. "Lola, I'm so excited! Finally, I get to get something I really want. Something I need."

Lola put a hand on her hip, then side-eyed Charly. "Yeah, and it's about time too. Who can forget the computer incident? Brigette knows she's wrong for that. Who steals their kid's computer money and never even apologizes or buys them one?"

Even though the mention of Brigette's "borrowing" the money Charly had saved for a computer would have ruffled her before, today she couldn't be moved. On this day, she would get her phone, and that device was way better than any PC, as far as she was concerned. Now she could connect to the world, study, act, and not have to hide the clunk of a cell she'd been forced to have, the one she was too ashamed to let anyone see, with the exception of her few close friends. "Opening it!" she said, ignoring Lola, and preparing them both for the big reveal.

Lola nodded, grabbing things out of the case before Charly had opened it all the way.

"Here," Charly said, moving the picture of her and her dad out of the way, then going for the rest. "The money's under here in a tear." The rubber-banded cue cards lay on the bed next to the case, as did notebooks. Finally, Charly stacked some loose papers on top of the pile.

"There. There it is!" Lola said, pointing to the slit. "I can see it."

Charly nodded, then did the same roundabout dance she'd done seconds ago. "Me too," she said, then stuck her fingers into the small opening. Her eyebrows cringed. Her fingertips touched only fabric and the shell of the suitcase. She grimaced, still feeling for the money. "It must've moved. Maybe it's farther down. . . ."

"Could've shifted when we moved it," Lola added, then began emptying more stuff out of the suitcase.

Finally, the suitcase was empty, and Charly could see the entire lining. It was just as flat as one of the pieces of paper she and Lola had set on the bed. Maybe she had folded it that thin, she tried to convince herself, sticking her hand farther inside the slit, feeling and hearing it rip. Still nothing.

"Let me help," Lola said.

Charly pushed Lola back. "I got this," she said, pulling her hand out of the slit and grabbing the tear. With all her might, she ripped the lining out of the suitcase. It was empty. There was not a dollar—not even a hint of money there. Stunned, Charly just stood looking into the bare suitcase. A tear trickled out of her eye; then she broke. Her head was in her hands, her feet were stomping on the floor, and a wail escaped her mouth, turning into a scream.

Stormy burst through the door. "What's wrong?" She looked at Lola, then Charly. "Oh God. What did Brigette do? I knew it. I knew it!" Stormy cried.

Charly's head perked. She knew her mother had gotten

her money, but hearing Stormy's confirmation incensed her. "What did she do, Stormy? What did you see?"

Stormy looked into Charly's teary eyes. "The casino. She rushed out of here to go to Elgin, and I knew something was wrong. How can you go to the boat casino if you're broke?"

Charly's head dropped, then her hand. She dug into her pocket and pulled out her ancient cell phone. Before she knew it, she had Brigette on the line.

"What'cha want?" Brigette said. "I can't be on here long; I'm not supposed to be on the phone on the floor."

"Where's my money, Brigette?" Charly yelled.

Brigette was quiet.

"You lost it? You lost it, gambling?!" Charly screamed, too mad to care about respecting her mother. "You owe me—"

Brigette's voice rose. "I don't owe you jack, Charly! If anything, you're trifling behind owes me for having you."

Charly hung up the phone before Brigette could say anything else. She looked at the suitcase with the ripped lining, then to Lola, and finally at Stormy. Her eyes moved back to the bed, then shot to the top of the open closet, and traveled down to the baggage on the floor. The beige one was too heavy, but somewhere in that stack of cases on the floor, one or two would do, and Charly knew which ones. Brigette's coveted lavender and natural leather set. "I'm not doing this anymore. It's my life, and I'm gonna make it what I want," was all Charly said before she took Brigette's luggage from the back of the closet, then began stuffing her belongings in it. "I'm going to move to New York and live with Auntie," she stated, then beamed despite being upset. "They're holding auditions for a reality show that's filmed at the network where she works."

"You think she'll let you?" Stormy asked, tears in her eyes.

Charly nodded. "Yes. She told me I could live with her years ago. Why not now?"

# 7

Mason was on Charly's left, and Stormy and Lola were in the seat behind her. Her bags—that's what they were now, hers, not Brigette's—knocked against the trunk of the SUV as they made their way down the pothole-riddled street heading toward Rockford, the nearest and second-largest city in Illinois. Charly leaned against the window and stared at the passing blocks. Everything looked a bit different to her now that she was leaving. The store on the corner where she'd shopped since she was a kid seemed small-town, nothing like the ones she imagined in New York, and the kids playing on the corner caused her to hurt. If they didn't leave like she was they'd be doomed, she believed.

"You okay?" Mason asked, putting his hand on her knee as he made his way onto Business Route 20.

Charly's eyes turned to face him before her head.

Mason snatched away his hand. "I'm sorry. I didn't mean . . ." he explained, mistaking Charly's look.

Charly smiled and shook her head. She waved away his explanation, not wanting to make him feel uncomfortable right before she left. She shrugged, looking longingly at him. She liked Mason too much to confuse him, and it was time he knew how she felt.

"Now or never," she mumbled, giving herself a pep talk. "It's okay, Mason. Really," she said, grabbing his hand and putting it back on her knee.

Mason glanced at her with stretched eyes, before putting his attention back on the road. The corners of his mouth turned up as he suppressed a smile. "Really," he parroted, then threw her a winking glance. "Like that?"

Charly nodded. "Like that," she confirmed.

Mason squeezed her knee. "You know you're dead wrong for telling me this when you're leaving, Charly. It's messed up." He zoomed down East State Street, then hung a left onto Mills Road, passing a gas station. He turned again, pulling into the parking lot of The Clock Tower Inn. The SUV cruised to a stop in front of the entrance, where Charly would wait for the bus to take her into Chicago.

Lola cleared her throat, then said, "Me and Stormy are going to get some snacks out of the gas station. It seems you two need to talk." She was quiet for a moment. "Isn't that right, Stormy? Stormy!"

Stormy, staring ahead at her sister and Mason, finally snapped to attention. "Um. Yeah. Right."

Mason looked intensely at Charly, then opened his door and hopped out of the SUV. He adjusted his fitted baseball cap, then stuck his hands in his pockets. "I'll get your bags."

Charly's eyebrows drew together. *What on earth was he talking about?* she wondered. Lola and Stormy had just given them time alone, and he'd opted to get her luggage instead of talking? That wasn't going to happen. She'd stayed quiet about her feelings for Mason for too long to just let their opportunity slip.

"Mason? You okay?" she asked, stepping down from the SUV and heading toward him.

He was setting her biggest suitcase on the ground. "Yeah. I'm good." His words were clipped and his expression was blank. He reached into the hatch to get the other, then drew back, obviously changing his mind. "You know what? I take that back. No, I'm not. I'm not good, Charly. And you're foul," he said, picking up her bag from the ground, then putting it back into the hatch. "Get in," he ordered, then went to the driver's side and waited for her to get in before he pulled off, then parked in the lot.

Charly just sat there. For once in her life, she was speechless. She was almost afraid to speak, fearing what Mason would say. She'd never seen him this way before, and it concerned her. "What is it, Mason? Why are you so mad?"

Mason's temples throbbed and he chewed on his bottom lip. He looked at her, half angry and half something else she couldn't pinpoint. "You know why I always track you down? Why I always talk to you? Or the reason that I borrowed this car—without permission—to take you to the bus so you can leave?"

Charly's eyes widened this time. She shook her head, then nodded. "Because we're friends who have so much in common?"

Mason chuckled. "No. Because I like you . . . as more than a friend."

Charly, still sitting, managed to put her hands on her hips. "Yeah, right. You like your friend who helped you with the paper," she accused.

Mason mushed her forehead.

"Ow!" Charly said. "Why'd you—"

Mason laughed coolly, but very calm. "Never that! My friend is my homeboy. We cool, but we're not that cool. Know what I mean?"

So Mason wasn't secretly seeing someone else. Relief moved through Charly, then quickly gave way to tension. With her moving almost a thousand miles away, it didn't matter if Mason was single or not. She'd be too far to have a serious relationship. "Well, I . . ."

Mason's lips were on hers before she could finish her sentence, and she didn't know whether to kiss him back or flee. As popular as she was, she'd never locked lips with someone before, and had found no one worthy of more than a casual cheek smooch. But Mason was different and more than worthy, she decided, then kissed him back.

"Here," he said, cutting short the kiss and putting a piece of paper in her hand. "That's my cousin's number in Brooklyn. When you get to the city, give her a call if you need anything." He pecked her on her lips again. "And call me if you need anything else, before you get there or after. I don't know why you just don't have your pops fly you out instead of taking the stupid bus."

Charly just stared into his eyes. Now would've been the perfect time to admit to lying about her father, but she couldn't come clean. Not after Mason had admitted to liking her too. She couldn't risk losing him so soon.

"It's just something I have to do on my own," she said, a mixture of excited and hurt. She was happy to leave, but she'd miss Stormy and Lola and Mason and her friends at Smax's. "And I don't want anyone stopping me."

Mason nodded, then arched his back, lifting his body from the seat. He stuck a hand in his pocket, and pulled out a thin stack of money. "I was gonna use this to buy some new kicks, but I figure you could use it more than me right now. I can't have my girl on the road without enough cash. And promise me you'll be careful."

Charly could see Lola and Stormy in the side mirror, approaching in the distance. Lola was smiling and talking a mile a minute and Stormy looked like someone had just died. A tear escaped Charly's eye. She'd miss her sister and worry about her constantly, but she had to leave. Her leaving was Stormy's only chance for happiness. Charly would go to New York, become a huge television star, then send for her sister. That was the plan, and it was also the promise she'd written to Stormy in the letter in her pocket. Hesitantly, she took the money from Mason. With only the one hundred dollars that she'd picked up from Bathsheba, she wasn't in the position to turn any cash down. "Thanks, Mason. You don't know how much this is going to help me."

Mason wiped away her tear, then got out of the SUV. He unloaded the trunk while Charly got out and met her sister and Lola halfway. By the time she reached Stormy, her dollar-store mascara was showing its worth, tracking down her cheeks in a black mess.

"Eww," Lola said, wiping Charly's face. "How're you gonna go grab anyone's attention for a reality show looking like this? Now if you were auditioning for Animal Planet, you'd be in, sister girl. Because right now you're resembling a raccoon. And it's not a good look for you."

Stormy smiled a huge, obviously false smile. "She's right, Charly. It's not the time to let yourself fall off. You're too pretty for that, and, remember, we're from the South Side."

Charly nodded, then wrapped her arms around Stormy. She held her tight, kissing the side of her head as if she'd birthed her while reaching into her pocket to retrieve the letter for Stormy.

"I got it, Stormy. I got it. You know I'm Charly St. James. I don't fall off, I make things happen," she said, then laughed, releasing Stormy from her embrace. "Here," she said, extending her instructions for Stormy. "Bathsheba will save your money for you, Smax will feed you, and this girl named Rebecca at the pet salon is holding a position for you. Don't worry about being too young for a job or working too hard. Nothing is going to get in the way of your studies. I told you I got this. . . . Well, I got you too." It was more truthful than she'd ever been.

"Hey!" Mason yelled. "Your bus is pulling in."

Charly looked at Stormy one more time, then turned

to a nodding Lola. "Let's go before you change your mind," Lola urged. "There's nothing here for you. And you don't have to worry about Stormy or Mason. I'm your eyes and ears, remember?" she asked, grabbing Charly and Stormy by their hands, then running toward the bus.

The doors of the bus were open and everyone else had boarded. Charly gave a third round of hugs, sure that she was going to miss everyone and promising to call them along the journey. Stormy dug into her jeans pocket and handed Charly her money.

"I think we should all give her what we have," she said, looking at Lola and Mason.

Mason nodded. "Me too."

Charly warmed, happy to see them all so supportive. "Mason already did, but you guys don't have to. Really."

Stormy shoved the money at Charly. "Take it." She looked at Lola, who stood there with her arms crossed and her lips poked out. "Lola?"

Lola stomped her foot. "Dag. Charly, I love you like a sister, but I told you I don't share my food or the last of my money." She paused.

Charly crossed her eyes at Lola. "You don't have to give me your money, Lola. I understand."

Stormy pushed Lola, and Mason looked at her like she had four heads.

"Okay. Okay. Dag!" Lola said, digging into her purse. She held out her hand to Charly. "Here. But you better pay me back when you get that TV gig."

Charly opened her palm, and Lola gave her twenty-six cents.

"Really, Lola?" everyone asked in chorus.

Lola rolled her eyes and sucked her teeth. "I didn't say I had a lot of money. I just said I hate giving away my last. All I had was a quarter and a penny." She reached into her shirt, moved her fingers around, then took out a piece of fabric. "But here," she said, handing Charly a handkerchief. "Pin the money to your bra, that way no one can steal it."

"Lola?" Charly protested.

Lola eyed Charly, then Stormy and Mason added their verbal agreement to Lola's demand. "Okay. Okay," Charly said, taking the money they'd given her, wrapped it in the handkerchief, then pinned it to her bra. "Better now?"

The bus driver cleared his throat, and Charly knew her time had come. She was on her way to make a new life for herself, and excitement shot through her veins. "Okay," she said to everyone. "I gotta go. I'll call you when I get to Chicago, then let you know which route I'm taking."

Charly climbed on board, then took one last look over her shoulder. She would miss Illinois but not enough to stay. "New York, here I come."

# II

## (some) <u>NOT</u> so
## v
## BEAUTIFUL FIASCOS

# 8

Charly's eyes stretched at the sight of the passengers. They varied in looks and cleanliness and age, she noticed as she made her way down the aisle, happy to be on her way. She plopped down into an available seat, one that was far enough away from anyone who appeared to be dirty or shifty. A smile spread and she nodded. The doors had closed, the bus had pulled off, and Charly was ready for her greatest adventure yet. She was headed to New York to move in with her aunt, find her dad, and snag two of her dreams: landing a spot on television and becoming Daddy's girl again. Or at least she thought she was. About fifteen minutes into the ride, a horrid smell lingered in the air, a stench so strong she swore it was drifting above her, mistlike, like in a fabric softener commercial. She covered her nose for fear the rankness would shoot up her nostrils and strangle her with funkiness. Her stomach turned, and the bus cruised and bounced and jerked, making her already uncomfortable feeling vamp into full-blown queasiness. Charly looked left, and the swaying cornfields made her dizzy. Closing her eyes, she stilled herself, waiting for the feeling to pass. She opened her lids and turned to the right, and someone's huge dented rear end was only inches from her face. The person, bent over, had on faded salmon-colored polyester pants, complete with an elastic waistband. Worse yet, the person's butt crack showed.

"Umph," Charly grunted, certain that she could smell what she was seeing, and, sure enough, to her stomach's dismay, flagrant booty odor assaulted her nose. Charly was certain she was only seconds away from throwing up in her own mouth. Her hand was clasped over her lips before she knew it. Her arm was through the handles of her tote and on the back of the seat hoisting her up while her feet were planted firmly on the floor helping her catapult to a stand.

"Excuse me!" Her yell, muffled by her hand, came out loud and strong as she pushed past the perpetrator of stink, then hustled her way down the narrow aisle toward the bathroom in the back.

Charly had never been so disgusted before. She stood in the tiny cubicle of a restroom, surrounded by a much worse smell than she'd run from. Her insides lurched, and she didn't know whether to toss her cookies standing erect or bending forward. If she vomited while she stood, it'd get all over her clothes and the tote bag. If she bent over the disgusting excuse for a toilet, she was certain she'd die. The metal bowl hadn't been flushed properly, and wads of used—skid-marked—toilet paper were inside and on the seat. Charly's head bounced on the wall behind her, thanks to the bus jerking. Deciding it was too late to be concerned about dirt or lice or God only knew what other kind of infestations from the wall, she leaned against it, pulled the collar of her shirt up over her nose, and tried to settle herself, breathing in her own perfume. She was on a mission. She would succeed. If she wanted to be on prime-time television, surely she could pull off a bus ride. Those were the things she told herself, but her stomach didn't have ears to hear, and it continued to turn.

A banging on the door made her forget why she was there. Suddenly her heart raced and her stomach stopped turning. She'd never been on a commuter bus alone, and the rapping stiffened her. She wondered if the minutes she'd been in the lavatory were beyond normal bus etiquette.

"Little girl? Little girl, you almost done? You okay in there?" a woman's voice asked.

Charly straightened her shirt, hoisted the tote over her shoulder, then opened the door. A pleasant face and, thankfully, a flowery scent of an elderly woman greeted her. Charly guessed the lady had to be in her late sixties. "I'm finished," Charly said, then thought about it. "But I wouldn't go in there if I were you. It's nasty and it stinks." She held up her hands in surrender. "And it wasn't me. I swear."

The elderly lady smiled, revealing too perfect dentures. She nodded. "I'm sure. But I didn't come to use the restroom. I came to check on you. You seem . . ." She put her index finger to her lip. ". . . well, let's just say as a mother of five and grandmother of twelve, and with the experience I've had in my seventy-two years, I can kinda tell you've never rode the 'Hound by yourself before. I just wanted to make sure you were all right. You know, with traveling alone and all."

Charly returned the smile, glad to have met a caring person, especially an older one. Her life had taught her that she could trust senior citizens. "I'm fine. I was a little queasy from the smell and other things," she said, deciding to keep the butt crack part to herself. "And thank you for checking on me. You're right; I've never traveled alone before," she added as the woman began to make her way back up the aisle. Charly followed and stared. The nice elderly woman had on faded salmon polyester pants with an elastic waistband.

The butt odor had been her imagination, Charly realized as she sat across the aisle from the elderly woman, who smelled of cheap flowers and had insisted Charly call her Grandma Anna. Smiling and relieved, Charly felt an immediate connection to the old lady and found herself telling Grandma Anna her entire life story. She was as comfortable with her as she'd been with all the other elderly people in her life, namely the crew at Smax's.

"So your momma took all your money? That's awful. Just awful. I don't know what's gotten into these chillun calling themselves parents nowadays. Mommas stealing from daughters. Lawd." Grandma Anna shook her head, then rubbed her hand on the worn Bible on her lap, which she referred to as her insurance policy. "Good God up in heaven," she declared, raising her hand in the air and closing her eyes. "Stealing? And from such a good child too? Put your hand on her, God. Cover and protect Charly with the blood of the lamb, and make sure she goes Your way because she's not her momma's child, she's Yours."

Though it felt strange, Charly closed her eyes and listened to Grandma Anna's prayer as warm tingles traveled up her spine, then wrapped around her bladder and squeezed. She had to pee. Badly. But there was no way she was going to the lavatory again.

"Amen," she repeated after Grandma Anna, signaling the session was done. "And thank you. Again. But—" Charly perked up and smiled, patting the tote that held her purse, where she'd put the hundred Bathsheba had given her, and tried to forget that she had to go to the bathroom. "Brigette didn't take all my money, just what I stashed in the old suitcase. Luckily for me, I still had my money from the restaurant, and my friends and sister gave me what they had before I left."

Grandma Anna nodded, and a warm feeling covered her wrinkled face. "I'm so happy to hear it. That's good, baby. A real good thing for them to do." She reached into her oversized pocketbook, pulled out a handful of peppermints and butterscotches, then proffered them to Charly. "Have one?"

Charly nodded, then selected two butterscotches. She wiggled in her seat. "Mind if I take two?"

Grandma Anna laughed. "Of course not, baby." She winked. "But it's gonna cost you." She laughed.

Charly laughed at the joke as the bus jerked to a stop at the Amtrak station in downtown Chicago. "We're already here," Charly exclaimed, unable to believe they'd arrived so soon, but happier than ever. Now she could start the next leg of her trip and free her bladder. She grabbed her purse, jumped up, and was making her way toward the exit before she knew it. She needed to be one of the first to collect her luggage from the driver so she could get to the restroom. Suddenly, she stopped. She was in such a rush to relieve her bladder and get to the train that would take her to New York that she'd forgotten about her new friend who couldn't move as fast as she. Grandma Anna. She turned, excused herself, and zigzagged her way between the passengers who'd lined up behind her, and made her way back.

"I'm sorry for leaving you, Grandma Anna," she said, peering around a couple of heftier people she couldn't squeeze by. "Stay there. I'm coming to help you off."

Grandma Anna waved and smiled her warm smile. "You gotta learn to worry about yourself, Charly. I know it sounds selfish, but I learned long ago that sometimes in this here world, that's the only way to make it. Look out for yourself." She nodded. "And with the journey ahead of you, you'll learn it too. Fast. Trust me on that. God helps those that help themselves. I'll meet you outside."

Charly couldn't remember ever seeing so much activity in her life. She tightened her grip on her wheeled luggage with one hand, and on Grandma Anna's arm with the other. She held the elderly lady to keep her steady and away from the riffraff she spotted while searching for a restroom sign. The Amtrak station was crowded with people moving to and fro, bumping into one another and not excusing themselves, and, to her surprise, innumerable homeless people. Her eyes widened. She'd never seen so many people without homes before. Her Midwestern hometown, though not a silver-spoon community, had very few down-and-outs, and she'd never seen people living in cardboard boxes, pushing shopping carts filled with what looked like trash, or standing on milk crates waving their respective religious books, damning everyone to hell for not feeding them.

"It's okay, child. You don't have to hold me so tight. I'm pretty spry," Grandma Anna assured, then pointed to an open waiting area. "There. We can sit over there," she said.

Charly wheeled her luggage, one bag belted to the other, and shook her head. There were two sections of seats facing each other, but not one was empty. Worst of all, there was not a bathroom sign in sight. She danced in place. "There's no room."

Grandma Anna unhooked her arm from Charly's. " 'Tis so. Watch this," she said, still headed to the occupied seating.

Charly followed, watching and wiggling. She had no idea how Grandma Anna planned to pull it off, but something told her the old lady would. Nearing the waiting area, her eyes widened when she saw where Grandma Anna was standing and whom she was talking to.

"Wow," she said, looking at the guy facing Grandma Anna. From where she stood, he looked like a painting. He had flawless skin, a nice shirt, and dark jeans covering long legs. He turned in her direction at the obvious insistence of Grandma Anna, who was pointing her way, and nodded and smiled. Seeing opportunity to flirt unfolding, Charly wiggle-walked right up to Grandma Anna's side, eavesdropping and taking in the oh-so-beautiful boy all while looking for a place to relieve herself.

"You seem like such a nice young man," Grandma Anna said to the guy, then looked over at Charly. "And this here is the sweetest girl in the world, the one I was just telling you about. What's your name, son?"

"Solomon," he said, then stood. Looking down at Charly, he licked his lips, then half smiled. "Pardon me," he excused himself, stepping out of Grandma Anna's way while his eyes were still on Charly. "Take my seat, miss."

"Grandma Anna," Charly said, mistaking Solomon's statement for a question. "And I'm Charly."

Solomon gave a slight head nod. "Charly. I know, she told me."

Charly gritted her teeth and begged her knees not to give. Cute or not, Solomon couldn't stop her bladder from needing to be relieved. "Whew" accidentally escaped her, and her eyes darted around.

"Child, go to the bathroom already," Grandma Anna said. "I'mma be fine right here. Don't you worry 'bout me. Just set your stuff here." She scooted over in her seat, allowing room for Charly's small tote, and pointed to the floor in front of her. "Nobody's gonna bother your suitcases with me here."

Charly nodded, then shook her head as she danced in place. "Okay. Solomon? Do you know where the bathrooms are?" She set her tote next to Grandma Anna and wheeled the bigger attached suitcases in front of her.

Solomon took Charly by the hand. "No disrespect, but it's the only way we're gonna part this sea of people. Together. Come on," he said, then pulled her through the crowd.

In the bathroom Charly splashed water on her face, then dried her hands. She may've been traveling, but she still wanted to look her best. Especially because Solomon was waiting for her outside. She fixed her eyebrows, then noticed how shiny her face was. Reaching for her purse to take out her blot powder, she realized it wasn't on her shoulder, it was in the tote. She shrugged. If this Solomon guy was interested, he'd be interested with or without her using blot powder to get rid of the shine on her forehead. "Maybe not," she told herself when she walked out of the bathroom, and he was nowhere to be found.

"Hey," Solomon said when she went back to the waiting area. He smiled big and wide. "I'm supposed to look out for you," he informed her.

Charly crinkled her brows together. "Huh?"

Solomon got out of the seat he'd let Grandma Anna sit in. "Go ahead and sit. I'm good standing."

Charly sat, looking around. "I still don't understand. What do you mean you're supposed to look after me? Where's Grandma Anna?"

"Well, your grandmother had to go. Said something about you and her going in different directions, and, oh, she said to tell you you're all paid up." He shrugged. "She said you'd figure it out."

Charly's eyebrows drew together. "Huh? What? I don't understand. Is that all she said?"

Solomon scratched his head. "She said something about a second butterscotch, and to remind you that God only takes care of those who take care of themselves."

Charly's heart raced and dropped. Her head turned left, then right, looking for Grandma Anna. Then her attention turned to the bags in front of her. *One. Two*, she counted. The wheeled ones set where she'd left them, give or take an inch or two, and her purse setting on top. The tote bag was gone. Charly blinked slowly, knowing something was wrong. She gulped, grabbed her purse, but was afraid to look inside. But what choice did she have? she questioned, picking it up and unzipping it. She took out her wallet, and saw everything was in its place. Identification. Pictures. Folded pieces of paper. All was there. All except the money. Where the cash once was, there was a note in its place.

---

1 PIECE OF BUTTERSCOTCH—$100.00

BILL PAID IN FULL

---

# 9

Charly banged her hand on the counter. She couldn't have been hearing correctly. Not today, not now. Raking her fingers through her hair, she batted back tears. "So there are no other seats?" she asked the reservationist, who'd been less than accommodating, and certainly didn't seem to like her job.

The lady, dressed in a dull uniform, popped her gum like a streetwalker and scratched her needed-to-be-tightened braids with overly designed acrylic nails. "Look. I just told you, and I'm not telling you again. All ninety-seven-dollar seats are booked. For days. Now if you want to go to New York today, it's gonna cost one-hundred-ninety-five dollars."

Charly nodded, feeling a bit better. If she could leave tomorrow, it wouldn't kill her to stay overnight in the train station. She'd heard of people bunking in airports all the time, so how much different could it be? A bum walked by, and his presence and stench explained the difference. But she didn't care. She was Charly St. James, and she'd survived Brigette, so she could and would handle anything. "Okay. So how about tomorrow? I want to book a ninety-seven-dollar ticket for tomorrow."

"Uh. Let me see," the rude reservationist said, then paused for a second as if in thought. "No! And no again. I told you, all ninety-seven-dollar seats are gone. Today, tomorrow, the day after, yadda, yadda, yadda." She leaned forward, resting her arms on the counter. "And before you ask, the difference is a twenty-hour straight ride versus a long ride with a layover in between. Oh, and business class." The woman rolled her eyes at Charly, then dismissed her with, "Next! Can I help the next passenger?"

The dirty sidewalk was under her feet and her remaining two suitcases were behind her before Charly knew it. She didn't know where she was going or how she was going to get there, but she would. And from that "didn't know where" she'd make it to the Big Apple. That, she was sure of. Vehicles blurred by, her shoulder bumped against people walking in the opposite direction, and the wind was to her face. She didn't care. Anger and hurt fueled her determination. Now she didn't just hate her hometown; she couldn't stand the whole state. Her pride in hailing from the South Side, as if it were her coat of arms, lost all valuable meaning.

"Where are you rushing off to?" Solomon asked, appearing from behind.

Charly looked at his legs and decided they were longer than she'd believed. Here she was hustling, moving as fast as she could without running, and he was keeping up with her without breaking a casual stride. "I'm getting out of here. I hate it here!" she ranted, still moving.

"Where is here?" he asked, his arm suddenly holding her back from entering a busy intersection and getting run over by cars zooming through the green light. "Slow down. It can't be that bad. Not bad enough to die."

A crowd was gathered at the corner, encircling them like a crescent moon, but Charly didn't notice. "Die? Who said anything about dying?" A gust of polluted air whooshed in her face, courtesy of the tailpipes belonging to a huge oil truck. A vehicle that she would've walked right in front of if it weren't for Solomon, she realized. "Point taken, but you're mistaken. I love myself too much for that—*and* to stay here. And the here I'm referring to, for your information, is *here*! Chicago. Illinois. The middle of nowhere."

Solomon nodded. The smile he'd worn before was now replaced with quiet strength. He had no words, and his face was minus expression as his eyes bore into hers.

"I'm tired of cornfields, bootleg mothers who can't see past working at car factories or men with thick wallets, and thieves . . . let's not even speak of the thieves," she began, her venting turning into a rant. Another truck zoomed by, almost-black smoke spurting from a stout on top that resembled a train from another century. She stomped her foot. "And all this friggin' pollution!" she yelled.

With a quick motion, Solomon pulled her into his arms. "Shh."

Charly tussled, past angry, beyond hurt and disappointed. "Let me go!" she yelled, her face pressed to his chest. "Let. Go," she begged at first, then gave way to her emotions and relaxed. She couldn't remember ever being held before by anyone except her dad, and that she couldn't even be sure of. The memory could've been a dream like so many others she'd imagined until they seemed so real that she couldn't distinguish fantasy from truth.

"Shh," Solomon said again. "It's going to be all right."

Charly stood there in his arms while passersby made their way around them without complaint. She hadn't realized how big and imposing he was until that moment, and, for minutes, she felt safer than she ever had. No longer did she worry about being robbed or how she was going to make it to New York. With Solomon, she just knew that it was all possible.

Solomon released her. "Better now?"

She nodded, then pursed her lips together. "Depends," she admitted, needing to be sure that her feeling was genuine and not something her imagination made her believe. "Aren't you supposed to be going somewhere too? I mean, you were in the train station."

He half smiled. "I'm already here. I just got in from New York, and was waiting for my folks to pick me up." He shrugged. "A funeral."

Charly nodded, sad about his reason for visiting what she now considered the prison she was trying to escape— the Midwest—and able to empathize. She was more familiar with death than she'd ever been. As she was stuck without enough money for a train or plane to take her to her destination, life was trying to kill her dream. She wouldn't allow it though. Not so easily. She forced a smile, telling herself it'd be okay. There was some light in Solomon's words.

"New York, huh?" she asked rhetorically. "That's good. That's where I'm going . . . if I can find a way to get there for less than a hundred and ninety-five dollars."

He reared back his head, drew his brows together in disbelief, then spread his lips into a full smile. He waved his hand as if swatting a fly. "That's easy. There are plenty of ways to get to New York. I should know. I'm originally from The Chi, and I used to take the dragon wagon there all the time before I moved there."

Charly lit up. "Dragon wagon? Really? What is it and how far is it?"

Solomon scratched his head. "It's just a bus, and it's not too far. I remember it being on Went . . . something. Sorry, it's been a long time since I caught it. Call me Missouri; I can show you better than I can tell you," he said, meaning he couldn't prove what he was saying with words.

"Cool. I so appreciate it," Charly exclaimed, taking him literally. She grabbed his hand and pulled. "Which direction?"

Solomon stood like a strongly constructed temple and didn't budge. "I wasn't serious, Charly. It's an expression."

This wasn't happening, Charly told herself. There was no way that she was going to let Solomon and his knowledge slip from her grasp. He had what she wanted, and was certain she could offer him the same. "Please, Solomon. I can pay." She let go of his hand and reached inside her shirt, peeling back her bra. She had to get her money.

"Okay. Okay," he said, staring at her exposed skin. "I'm sure it's a nice view, but there's no need to strip out here on the street." He grabbed her arm, stopping her, then took his phone out of his pocket. "I'll just have my folks pick me up from there. I'm sure they remember where it is."

They'd walked down South Canal Street, turned left on West Seventeenth, made a right on South Stewart, then made another left on West Eighteenth, then high-tailed it toward Wentworth Avenue, where the bus station was. Charly pressed SEND on her phone. She'd texted Stormy and Lola and Mason her every move just in case something went wrong. The dragon wagon bus station, as Solomon had called it, was located in the heart of China-town near Chinatown Square, Charly discovered, her eyes wide from all the sights. They were by the Three Happiness restaurant and Chinatown Market, not far from the fire department. The hike was long in thought, but quick in travel. She assumed they couldn't have walked more than two miles, but it'd taken them almost forty-five minutes.

She looked around, eyed the chain-link fence behind the building. From her view, all she could see was discarded litter lining it, and it looked like it had once held a parking lot. To her right was a busy intersection with Chinese architecture on one side and, on the other, was the Red Line Cernak-Chinatown train stop for commuters traveling to 95/Dan Ryan. She nodded. So it wasn't the airport or the Amtrak. It wasn't even a semblance of a

Greyhound facility. The dragon wagon bus station wasn't really a bus station at all, she discovered. It was just an office housed in a painted red brick building.

"Where does the bus pick up?" she asked.

Solomon laughed. "Right there," he said, pointing to the street. "Curb service at its best." He shrugged. "You get what you pay for, right? Let's go in and get you settled." He led her through the red door, then whipped out his iPhone and began texting. "My fam," he explained, then paused, looking at the cell screen. "They're a couple blocks away, but it's cool though. I won't leave you until I know you're good."

Once Solomon was outside with her bags, and not a man was in sight, Charly fished out the cash from the handkerchief pinned to her bra, not caring who saw what. She was safe, and her time had come.

"One ticket to New York. First class!" she joked to the woman at the counter, knowing classes didn't exist on buses. Or did they? she wondered when the surprisingly tall Chinese lady began punching keys on a computer.

"That'll be one-hundred-ten dollars. Date?" the lady asked in a crisp British accent, killing Charly's assumption that most people in Chinatown would be working with broken English.

Charly wasn't surprised. She wasn't in Small Town U.S.A. anymore and knew all sorts of stereotypes people believed weren't true. Just as all white people weren't good at baseball and all black people didn't shoot hoops, all Asian people didn't speak alike. People varied. She'd learned that in social studies class and from her friends of different ethnicities. Lola, for one, was a great example.

Who knew of a black girl born with natural ocean-blue eyes and extremely blond hair?

"Today. I'm leaving today," Charly said.

The Chinese lady shook her head. "The bus departs to New York on Sundays, Tuesdays, and Thursdays only. Let me check tomorrow's schedule." She began punching computer keys again, making Charly's hope rise. "I'm sorry." She shook her head. "I'm not sure what's going on on the East Coast, but we're booked for the week. Amazing. I've never seen this. . . ."

# 10

She could feel herself turning into one of the many homeless people the Illinois news stations were always broadcasting about on television. Exiting the makeshift bus station, she jetted full speed across the street toward the Red Line train. Digging into the bottom of her purse for the money she'd just put into it, she felt for change she knew wasn't there. She didn't know how much train fare was or where she was going, but she had to go somewhere. She couldn't just stay in Chinatown, and, as far as she was concerned, she had no home to return to. The only thing in front of her was space and opportunity. She was free to go wherever she wanted and take advantage of every good possibility life had to offer.

"Yo, Charly!" Solomon's voice called from behind. "Char-lee!"

Charly zipped around the back of a passing car, then

took a quick look over her shoulder. Solomon was standing on the other side of the street in front of the dragon wagon station. His hands were cupped around his mouth, and he was still calling her name. When her foot stepped onto the sidewalk and she knew she was safe from passing traffic, she turned. Solomon was so cute and helpful, but that wasn't enough to make her change direction. She didn't want him to think her ungrateful or, worse, someone who disappeared once they'd received what they wanted, but she didn't want to go backward. Backward was equivalent to past tense in her mind, and all she wanted to see now was what the future held for her. She shrugged her shoulders. "Sorry, Solomon!" she yelled, hoping he could hear her over the flow of traffic. "But I gotta go. No buses are leaving from there."

He was yelling something she couldn't make out when she entered the Red Line station. Other traingoers flanked both her sides, going through the turnstiles, then heading to the platform. She didn't know exactly where she was headed to, but there had to be another alternative to get her to New York. The dragon wagon couldn't be the only bus. "Here goes," she said, pulling out cash to pay the fare. Her heart dropped, then sped when she noticed there were no coin or dollar slots for her to insert the money. A sticker on the turnstile caught her attention.

---

Farecards only—main entrance 1 block south

CTA Red Line

---

Charly grimaced. She was no geographer or astrologer; she had no idea which direction was south. She shrugged, keeping the fare money in her hand, and ignoring the impatient complaints of a few people behind her.

"Okay," she said, looking to her left, then right. She knew what she was about to do would be considered wrong, but, to her, consider was the operative word. Her intentions were good and she had every intention of paying, and would do so. She'd just pay the fare to the first CTA employee she saw, then her entering without a fare-card wouldn't really be stealing. *Not at all*, she assured herself, putting her hands on the top of the turnstile and lifting her body over it.

Hands were gripping the back of her arm before she could jump the turnstile completely. "Come with me," a female Chicago transit cop said from behind, pulling her back.

Charly held out her hand once her feet were planted firmly on the ground. "Here. I have my fare right here. I swear."

"That's good," the small-framed female cop said. She was smaller than Charly in stature, but her presence was huge, especially because she carried a firearm. "I'm sure your mother will be happy to hear that. I'd just love it if my child had money to pay for something and then stole it," she said, walking through the turnstile herself, then sliding her arm through Charly's. She led her down a walkway to an inconspicuous door. "You just gave me something to do. I'm just getting here, and already I have paperwork to process, thanks to you."

"But—" Charly began to protest and explain.

"But nothing," the officer said, removing a key ring from a loop on her pants, then searching for one. "I can't believe this," she complained, still looking for a key. "I left it in the cruiser." She took a walkie-talkie from her hip. "I need assistance. . . ." she began, then went back and forth with whoever was on the other end. "Not locked? Really? Okay," she said. "I'll try it." She holstered her walkie-talkie, then turned to Charly. "Don't you move," she warned, then let go of Charly.

"Okay," Charly said, then watched as the officer pulled on the doorknob, struggling to get the stuck door open.

The officer held the knob with both hands, put the heel of her foot on the brick wall, then pressed her weight against it. The door rattled, but it was obviously very stuck. Charly watched as the officer struggled with the door, and admired the tenacity of the small cop. No matter how much the metal door refused to give, the cop didn't let up, but instead tried harder, muttering here and there. A loud noise, followed by a barrage of curses, sliced through the air, then glass bottles flew past Charly's head and crashed to the ground. Shards of glass flew and ricocheted everywhere. Charly ducked, barely escaping a cut or two, and saw a group of teenagers passing by with alcohol and cigarettes and bottles in their hands. They were yelling and singing and, obviously, inebriated.

Suddenly, she felt a burn on the back of her arm. "Ow!" she said, realizing that the glass had hit her.

"What the hell?" the officer said, looking at her arm. A

trail of blood moved from her bicep to just above her wrist. "Wait here. And don't you move," she said to Charly, whipping out the walkie-talkie with one hand and unlocking her firearm holster with the other.

Like a deer in headlights, Charly stood in place, afraid to move. She gripped her purse to her side, then thought better of it as more teens ran past, followed by a couple of adults who seemed to be running late. Chicago surely wasn't Belvidere, and was too dangerous to let her bag be so free. She took it off, draped the strap around her neck, fed one of her arms through it, and crisscrossed it over her midsection. One of her hands stayed inside it, keeping the money in her wallet safe. Yes, she still had a stash in her bra, but she needed all the cash she had. Teenagers still shuffled by, some loud and boisterous, others looking as innocent or intimidated as she. Her phone vibrated in her pocket, scaring her. She'd forgotten it was there.

"Hello?" she said breathlessly.

"Charly! What's good, baby girl?" Mason's smooth voice asked, giving her a dose of home that she needed.

"Baby girl?" Charly laughed, despite being so rattled. "That's a new one . . . but nothing's good, Mason. Nothing." She gave him a rundown of all her happenings, including waiting on the platform for the cop.

"Serious? You're waiting on the po-po to come get you?! Nah! Don't do that." He was silent for a moment. "Where's your ID?"

"In my purse. Why?"

Mason exhaled on the phone. "Listen to me, Charly. Listen to me carefully. You're a teenager, no one can search you without your ma dukes' permission. Hide your ID in your panties, and whatever you do, don't give them your government."

Charly's face twisted into a look of confusion. What was he talking about? "I don't get it." A group of cops now ran past her, one slowing down and looking back at her. "I think one's here to get me, Mason. He just turned around. Maybe the lady cop told him—"

"Don't give them your real name, Charly. That's your government, what's on your birth certificate. And hide your friggin' ID in your panties or bra, and don't talk. Don't say anything! You hear me? And if you give them any name, give 'em Brooklyn Mason. I'll be calling and checking, and if they detain you under that name, I'll be there to get you somehow."

The officer who'd slowed down and was looking at Charly was now clearly headed her way. He had a walkie-talkie up to his mouth, talking into it. From the look on his face, she knew he was coming for her. She gulped. "Another one's coming to get me."

"Power off your phone and do what I said. I got'chu, Charly. I got'chu. Remember Brooklyn Mason."

She was sliding her ID and powered-off phone into her panties and bra, respectively, as she walked with the tall male officer who'd snatched her up by one arm, and was semi-dragging her down the walk toward the exit of the station.

"So you like to throw bottles, huh?" he barked. "Juvie's got spots for trash like you." He pushed her through an entrance/exit door used for the handicapped and commuters with strollers.

Charly almost fell, and she wasn't happy about it. Mason may have given her good advice, but being shoved gave her temporary amnesia. This man, an officer of the law or not, couldn't just push her and get away with it. "You better keep your hands off me," Charly snapped. "Push me again and see what happens."

The cop yanked her by her arm, half drug her to a brick wall, then threw her against it. "A threat? And you have a smart mouth too? I'll show you what's going to happen."

Both of her hands were behind her back and cuffed before she knew it. Like a common criminal, she was escorted out of the station and to the end of the line of the group of juvenile offenders who'd thrown bottles and cut the woman officer. They were forced face-first against the wall. Chicago Transit Authority police cars and paddy wagon vans were parked on the street, and cops, transit authority and city, were gathered around. Some wore riot gear and had their guns exposed. Others had what looked like metal batons, and a few had cups of coffee and were laughing. Charly didn't understand what they thought was so funny when her life was crumbling.

"Turn to your left and stay in a straight line," one of them instructed Charly and the other teenagers. "Roger, how many do you want to a van?" the cop asked another.

Charly turned left and saw the woman officer who'd snatched her for jumping the turnstile. She bore her eyes into the lady, trying to get her to look at her. "Hey!" she yelled. "Hey! Tell them it wasn't me. I wasn't a part of this mess."

"Shut up. You're going with the rest of 'em," the officer who'd pushed her said.

"Wait, Kaminski," the female cop finally said, then pointed to Charly. "She wasn't with them. You can uncuff that one. She's not a runner, and we probably should have her checked out. I think she got cut too." She looked at Charly. "But you better not move until someone comes to get you. We have unfinished business."

Reluctantly Kaminski freed her wrists, then spat on the ground in front of her. "You're still a delinquent. Trash like you will never be nothing."

"Whatever!" Charly said, rubbing her wrists.

Locking up inebriated teenagers wasn't going to be an easy task, Charly realized. The offenders couldn't stand in a straight line or be quiet. Some yelled curses and insults; others just flat-out threatened the cops. The few who stood directly in front of her seemed to forget that they were going to jail. They started crunk dancing, jerking their bodies in all sorts of directions, while a few cheered them on, making music with their mouths.

"Do that ish. Do that ish. Do it!" someone sang from a small crowd of other teens who'd stopped to enjoy the crunk dance show.

"Disperse! Disperse!" some officer yelled to the decidedly deaf onlookers, while a couple of the bystanders became a part of the show that had become a competition.

Charly watched the whole thing play out in front of

her like a movie. The officer who'd snatched her for jumping the turnstile was in the middle of the block by one of the jail vans. Kaminski, the big dude who liked to shove teenage girls, was trying to settle the teenagers at the front of the line, pushing them, one by one, to another officer who was shoving them inside police cruisers and paddy wagons.

"Why are you still here?" one of the teenagers asked her, not turning all the way around.

"Huh?" Charly asked. "Turn around. I can't hear you."

"I can't. If I do, they'll know we're talking. You must be innocent. You're green." He paused as another officer passed them. "I said, why are you still here?"

Charly looked at the side of his face, wondering if he was drunk and crazy. Hadn't he heard the female officer tell her to stay put? "She told me to stay here," she said through clenched teeth to the side of his face.

"And the big dude said you were trash and would never be nothing. Is that true?" He turned quickly, gave her the side eye, then turned away.

"Uh, no!" Charly said.

"Get yo hands out my pocket!" the dude in cuffs suddenly yelled.

Charly looked at his pockets. No one had their hands in them.

"I said, get yo hands out my pocket!" he yelled again, swooping back his leg and kicking Charly's shin.

"Ouch," she whispered. "Why'd you kick me?"

Again he yelled at the top of his lungs for someone to get out of his pocket. Suddenly, like dominoes falling, the teenagers lined up in front of him began screaming the same thing. "Malcolm X," he said to Charly. "Think of the Malcolm X movie. A distraction . . ."

Charly paused for a second, trying to recall the scene in *Malcolm X* the boy was referring to. She nodded, finally understanding what he was doing. He was creating a distraction for her. The guy shouted for someone to get their hand out of his pocket again, making butterflies form in her stomach. She looked and saw no one was watching her. Her wrists were free of cuffs. "Thanks," she whispered, easing backward until she was less than three feet from the corner. Dipping around the transit building, she took off like an Olympic track star, her adrenaline pushing her faster and faster down the street and between buildings in Chinatown.

# 11

She'd zigzagged through buildings, turned corners, and was now in Chinatown's shopping district, Armour Square. The wind was to her back, pushing down the wide walk flanked by stores on either side. A red patterned rail lined the second floor of the outside mall.

The sound of feet hitting the pavement made her move faster. Her semi crime wasn't bad enough for the cops to give chase, so she didn't understand why she was being sought like a fugitive. She'd only jumped the turnstile until she could find someone to give her fare to, and hadn't really seen a problem with it. She'd meant well but, obviously, Chicago police didn't care.

A red-and-white sign with Chinese and English on it caught her attention. WJ Bookstore had a selection of books in the window, and she could see a few people through the glass. Afraid to turn around, Charly pulled open the door, then stood on the side of it, heaving and peering out to see if the cops were coming after her.

"Can I help you?" an older man asked, his accent strong, standing behind the counter.

Charly bent forward, her hands on her knees, and tried to catch her breath. A bunch of kids ran by laughing and playing. One was on a skateboard. She exhaled. So it hadn't been the police, she thought. She'd become paranoid. "I'm okay," she smiled at the older man. "I was just looking for something to do a social studies project on. Culture."

The old man nodded, then turned away from her. "Let me know," he said, then picked up a newspaper.

Charly perused the few aisles of the store as if she intended to buy something. She'd never actually been in a Chinese store before, and found the selections interesting. A green bottle with Chinese lettering on it caught her attention. She picked it up, turned it over, and saw it had an English description on it.

> Chinese Green Tea. Ginseng. Stress Relief. Healthy Weight. Energy Enhancer. Best Concentrated Tea. Good for You!

Though she knew she had to save money, she needed more energy, and she needed relief from the stress she'd come to know in less than a day. On top of that, maintaining her figure for the television studio cameras would be a good thing too, she decided, taking the tea to the register.

"Dat all?" the man asked, ringing up her purchase.

She nodded, then thought better of it. "Does this really do what it says? And do you know if there's another bus around here that goes to New York?"

The man smiled. "Best, best tea. Strong. Portent." He held up a finger and pointed outside. "Bus on Wentworth take you to New York."

Charly paid for the tea, thanked the man, then made her way out. Her stomach growled as she passed Yin Wall City. There were so many restaurants around; she didn't know where to eat. Great Wall Restaurant was up on the left, and she noticed the B.B.Q. KING in the window. Barbecue reminded her of Smax's, and that's just what she needed. Reaching for the door, a voice stopped her.

"Char-lee!"

*Solomon?* Charly smiled, then turned. Solomon was stores away, his hands cupped around his mouth. "Solomon? What are you doing here?" she asked, turning away from the restaurant and moving toward him.

Solomon bent down, then stood holding up his hands. He laughed. With his right one he had her luggage. "So you don't need these?" He waved the bags to and fro, lowering them to the ground as he swung them.

Charly smiled and shrugged, hustling her way to him, breaking into a slow jog. At least now she knew Solomon wasn't a thief. He'd had plenty of opportunity to dip with her luggage, but he hadn't.

"Come on," he said as she approached him. "Me and my uncle have been looking for you. I thought I saw you hemmed up with the po-po, but then I thought *nah*. It couldn't be."

Charly nodded. "Yes. It was. I ran."

Solomon reared back his head. "Word? I guess you're more of a city slicker than you think," he said, leading the way.

"How did you know I was here?" she asked, moving her legs as fast as she could to keep up with his pace.

He shook his head. "I didn't. My unc wanted me to grab him something to eat, then we were going to go back to the bus stop, then Amtrak. Don't worry about it now, though. You're coming with us."

She stopped in her tracks. "To the funeral?"

Solomon laughed. "If you want. But I was talking about to my fam's house. They're hustlers. They can hustle their way out of and into anything. I'm sure they can get you to New York."

Relief whooshed through her. After a long trying day, she would finally be able to make some progress on her almost eight-hundred-mile journey. She took her luggage from him. "But if you were looking for me, why didn't you just leave my bags in the car until you found me?"

Solomon stopped in front of a take-out restaurant, then pulled open the door for her. "I just felt they were safer with me. Let's grab a bite. We have a long ride."

# 12

Solomon's uncle's passenger van was atrocious. Really over the top and ghetto to the nth degree. It was old school and beyond country. It was royal blue on the bottom, champagne on the top, and it had to have been made in the nineties, Charly thought. There were four lightly tinted windows on both sides with ALL THAT & A BAG OF CHIPS scrawled on them in gold. Inside there were raggedy drawback curtains on each window and prominent cup holders that swung around each seat, complete with pimpish drinking glasses that made Lil Jon's diamond-encrusted one seem infantile in platinum-and-bling comparison.

"Come on in, shorty doowop," a man—Solomon's uncle, Charly assumed—said. "Ain't nothing to it. See what I'm saying, shorty?"

Charly nodded to please him, grabbing hold of the

banister of the van's fold-out steps, then climbed the stairs to get inside. She handed him the plastic white bag with his takeout in it, then looked to the driver's seat, sure that he must fall under some classification of handicapped. What else could be the reason for stair steps in a vehicle? Then she thought better of it. If he was wheelchair-bound, he wouldn't be able to use the added feature. "Thanks for helping," she said in reply to his question. She wanted to tell him that, no, she had no idea what he was saying. Nor did she know what was to it.

Solomon laughed, getting in the van behind her. He adjusted her luggage in a seat behind them, then elbowed her slightly. He shook his head when their eyes connected. "My fam's a bit . . . well, uh. Different," he explained in a whisper. "But they're good people." He removed a cell plug from a book bag, connected it to his cell phone, then plugged it into the floor.

Charly smiled, following suit. The van may've been a bit over the top, but she could appreciate the electrical feature. She needed to juice her cell too. "I get that. More than you know," she admitted to Solomon. Her family—well, one person in her life—was a bit different too, but unlike Solomon's people, Brigette wasn't good.

"Buckle up, whoever you are. Name's Outlaw, in case you didn't know. Know why they call me Outlaw?" he asked, laughing. "Because I don't believe in laws. Speeding laws. Traffic laws. Which-side-of-the-street-I'm-supposed-to-drive-on laws. Oh, and don't let me forget, traffic-light laws. I'm too old to play red light, green light. See what I'm saying, shorty?" Outlaw turned to her, smiling. He had all his top and bottom front teeth, but huge gaps on the sides. Charly guessed if there was such a thing as dental laws, he definitely wouldn't believe in those either.

Her head banged against the headrest and her body jerked backward, slamming her small frame into the seat. Outlaw zoomed down West Twenty-second Street, swerving through traffic at full speed, banging on the steering wheel and cursing at every car in front of him. Without hesitation or caution, he veered onto the Dan Ryan Expressway, ignoring cars in his path and the blaring horns of angry drivers who didn't appreciate his almost running them off the road.

"Get outta the way! Outlaw's coming through," he yelled, removing his hands from the wheel once the Dan Ryan became I-94 E, and used his leg to steer the van.

Charly's eyes bulged when she realized that he planned on steering with his leg while he ate his takeout. She almost shot out of her seat when she saw Outlaw reach over to the passenger side, dig into a black plastic bag, and pull out a huge bottle of liquor. It had to be at least a gallon, she guessed as she watched him unscrew the top, hold it up to his readied mouth, then drink it like it was water. The amber-brown liquid lowered at least an inch as he gulped. She yawned, then remembered the green tea she'd purchased at the Chinese store. The label said it provided energy, and she hoped it was true because she couldn't go to sleep. Not with Outlaw drinking and driving.

She reached into the bag, took it out, then drunk it until the bottle was empty. She nodded toward Outlaw, who was taking a second swig of the alcohol. "You think that's a good idea?" she had to ask.

"It's cool," Solomon said, scarfing down his takeout like he hadn't eaten in days. "Unc is an alcoholic. If he doesn't drink, he can't function." He shrugged. "Believe me. You don't wanna see him sober. It's cool," he said again, which made her worry. "Here," he said, extending his Styrofoam container. "You want some fried rice, lo mein or barbecue pork? It's good." He licked his fingers.

"I'm okay," Charly said, her eyes on Outlaw as she ignored her empty stomach. She hadn't eaten and would've loved nothing more than to have a good meal, but she couldn't afford to take her eyes off Outlaw for that long. She yawned, then sucked her teeth in irritation. The green tea label had lied. It wasn't giving her energy and exhaustion was moving in, and it was too heavy for her to fight. But she was afraid to close her eyes.

"You sure we're okay?" she asked Solomon, who nodded. "Are you tired?" He stuck a plastic fork full of food into his mouth, shaking his head no. "I only need a quick power nap. Maybe twenty minutes," she said. "I'm tired."

Solomon nodded. "Go ahead. I'm up, and I ain't gonna let nothing happen. I swear, Unc does this all the time, and ain't never had an accident."

Staying awake for as long as she could manage, Charly watched the traffic from the curtained window next to her. They zoomed down the expressway, passing cars and trucks, leaving them behind like the trees flanking the highway. She inhaled deeply, breathing in the smells of takeout and alcohol until she didn't smell them anymore. A partial smile formed on her face. Yes, the ride wasn't what she'd planned, but at least she was on her way, she told herself, then gave in to the heaviness of her exhaustion.

"Aw. Aw. Oh God!"

Charly opened her eyes and grabbed onto the armrests.

"Oh. God. Stop! Stop!" Solomon yelled from the captain's seat next to her, one of his hands on an armrest, the other over his mouth. He was half standing and the color of his face was off. He was no longer brown, but grayish.

"What is it?" she asked, unbuckling her seat belt and scooting to the edge of her seat.

The van swerved, then jerked to a stop. From behind she could see Outlaw throw the gearshift in park and open the driver's door. He stuck his head out of the door, made a weird noise, then released the contents of his stomach onto the pavement. Charly winced. The color, the smell, the sound of splashing vomit sickened her. She turned her head toward Solomon.

"Oh—" he began. Then his insides pushed up and out of his mouth too, but he didn't have a door to open on his side of the van to stick out his head like Outlaw had. The takeout food he'd eaten earlier was now on the floor and running down the back of the driver's seat, looking like brownish pea-green baby poop.

Charly's hand was over her mouth and her stomach

was churning. She retched, but had nothing to throw up. "Oh," she said, then opened the door and hopped out. She paced, taking in the fresh air in quick spurts.

"Your turn," Outlaw said, meeting her on the side of the van, and wiping his mouth on the back of his shirt-sleeve. The bottle of liquor was in his other hand. He lifted it to his mouth, threw back his head, and took a long drink, audibly gulping. "Ahh," he said, then screwed the cap back on, signaling he was finished.

"My turn?" Charly questioned, then saw perspiration building on Outlaw's now-graying face. His complexion turned sullen, and almost immediately, he was bending forward, regurgitating all he'd just swallowed.

He heaved, and chunks of whitish goop hit the ground. "Your turn . . ." He continued to vomit. "Your turn to . . ."

"You're gonna have to drive, Charly," Solomon said, appearing from the other side of the van, and taking the same bent-forward position as Outlaw, and throwing up too. "I." Retch. "Think." Retch. "We." Double retch. "Got food poisoning."

Charly's heart raced. Food poisoning? No way. They couldn't possibly have that. Drunk, yes, she saw every reason for Outlaw to be so, but he couldn't be sick. Solomon also couldn't be ill. Neither one of them could be for safety's sake. "Maybe if we just stand here for a few, you guys will be okay. The air will help."

"Like hell!" Outlaw said between heaves. He retched loud and strong and long, then doubled over, holding his stomach.

"Yes, Charly. You have to drive." Solomon leaned

against the back of the van, wrapping his arms around his middle and grimacing.

"But I don't—" Charly began, trying to tell them that she didn't know how to drive, but was drowned out by the violent sounds of Outlaw and Solomon retching and vomiting, and Outlaw's cursing.

# 13

"It's easy," Stormy said, and Lola was in the background, backing Stormy's insistence up.

Charly connected her earpiece with the cell phone, and listened intently to her sister and best friend try to tell her how to drive Outlaw's van. "The key's in the ignition," she told them. "And I'm about to put it in drive," she warned, then looked over her shoulder at the now sleeping Solomon and Outlaw.

"Make sure you look for oncoming traffic in the mirrors," Stormy said, her voice coming through Charly's headset like her sister was right next to her.

"Yes. Do that!" Lola screamed, her mouth apparently next to Stormy's phone.

Charly nodded. She thought it sad and pitiful that she had to call home to get driving instructions, but she was too rattled to give it a go, and she needed to keep someone informed of her whereabouts. "How do you know all this stuff?" she asked her younger sister.

Stormy laughed. "The Internet. I'm at Lola's," she explained. "So, do you think you got it? I don't want you to talk and drive. It's too dangerous."

Charly nodded as if they could see her.

"Do you?" Lola asked.

"Yes," Charly said. "I got it. Buckle up. Check my mirrors for traffic. Put the van in drive. Ease into traffic. Use one foot," she said as she performed each of the things she said, step by step. She gripped the steering wheel tight, afraid to let go. "Hang up," she told Stormy and Lola. "Hang up because I can't. I'm driving! Can you believe it? I'm driving!" she exclaimed as she pulled onto the expressway.

"Okay!" Stormy yelled. "And don't forget to power off your phone. Remember you have to save battery time until you find a plug to charge it."

The line went dead before Charly had time to tell them it wasn't necessary. Her phone was fully charged, and so was her heart, she realized when she pulled into traffic and could hear its beat in her ears.

Cars and trucks now sped past her, blowing their horns and flipping her the bird. She looked at the dashboard. She was driving forty-five miles per hour, the minimum speed limit according to the sign she'd just passed, so she didn't see what everyone was so angry for. She shrugged, keeping her hands stiff on the wheel. If everyone was in such a hurry, they could just zip by her, she thought, then felt a stabbing pain in her stomach. It stopped as quickly as it had started, and it didn't worry her. Unlike Solomon and Outlaw, she hadn't eaten the takeout so she knew she didn't have food poisoning. A yellow light lit on the dash, pulling her attention for a second. The gas tank was almost empty. "Mmm," Charly said. Her stomach seemed to be knotting. A loud noise rumbled like she was digesting food. She shook her head, then saw a big blue sign. A rest stop was coming up in a few miles, and the picture showed symbols for food and gas.

A low, moaning noise came from the backseat. Charly turned her head for a second, then whipped it back around. She didn't have this driving thing down yet, and, for fear of having an accident, she was too scared to look long enough to see who was making the noise.

"Ugh," the sound came again, and Charly didn't know if it was from Solomon or Outlaw.

"Are you . . . ?" she began, then was cut short by her own stomach growling and hurting. She could feel the gas build in her stomach, and an intense heat warmed her from inside. She gulped. She'd felt this way before, but usually after eating broccoli or beans. "Ooh," she whispered, lifting up her bottom from the seat. She'd cut one, and hoped no one knew.

"What's that stanking?" Outlaw asked, half asleep. His voice sounded chalky. A smell, worse than the one Charly had just dealt, filled the air. His god-awful breath.

Charly reached over and let down the automatic window. Her phone almost fell from her lap, and she caught it, then stuck it in her pocket. The van swerved, zigzagged into another lane. In the side mirror, she could see a car jerk into another lane, right before it blared its horn at her. She shook her head. She'd almost crashed trying to air out the van and save her cell.

"I dunno," she lied, her stomach balling and aching. She had the worst case of gas ever, and had never felt pain so badly. Again, it slipped from her silently. She winced. It was so bad she couldn't take it.

"Oh. Ill." That was Solomon. "Roll up the window," he said.

"Smells like someone hit a skunk," Charly said, seeing the exit just up ahead. Her stomach grumbled, her gas bloating her small frame and making her sweat. She gripped the wheel, trying to hold it in. Without thought or fear of having an accident, she punched the accelerator. The van sped, bouncing along and over potholes. Outlaw and Solomon moaned in the back, but she didn't care. She had to make it to the gas station as quickly as she could. Never mind the tank needing to be filled, she needed to be emptied. Fast.

She skidded to a halt at the stop sign, forgetting if the station was to her left or right. The area was desolate, and there was nothing but trees and farms in her view. Charly shrugged, then whipped the van to the right and sped, looking for a gas station. She'd driven almost two miles, and still, nothing. Sweat now formed in bullet-sized droplets on her forehead, and tracked down the sides of her face. She could feel the gas pushing its way down to her pelvic area; then like someone had punched her, it made its way out, loud and strong.

Outlaw broke out into laughter from the back. "I knew it. That's you, Charly! You smell like somebody done crawled up in you and died!" He was silent for a second, then moaned again in pain. "I ain't never eating that mess again."

"Un-unh," she lied. "I don't know what that is. I must've ran over something."

There was nothing in front of her but open road; then she spotted a farmhouse in the distance. She'd make a U-turn there, she decided. If she hadn't seen a gas station yet, it had to be the other way.

"Mm-hmm," Outlaw said.

Charly looked in her rearview, saw that he'd fallen asleep and Solomon hadn't been awakened by her gas. She exhaled, relieved, then tensed up as fast as she'd relaxed. The gas was attacking her again. She shook her head. The farmhouse was only a few hundred feet away, but she didn't think she could make it, not with the way her stomach was bubbling. "Here we go," she said, slowing, then throwing the steering wheel all the way to the right, and punching the accelerator. The van shot down the road at over a hundred miles per hour.

In minutes, the filling station was in sight. Charly slowed and prepared to pull in when her stomach set fire again. She hit the accelerator to speed up, but had under-estimated the power of the van. She'd bypassed the entrance. "Dang!" she said, putting the gear in reverse, and pressing the gas again. Her stomach gripped her, and she threw the van in drive, turned the wheel to pull into the lot, accelerated, and drove straight into a ditch.

"What the . . . ?" Outlaw yelled.

Charly's head bounced off the steering wheel. Her hand grabbed the door handle. She pulled. Hopped out.

Dug her heels in the ditch and pushed her way up and out. She ran like she was on fire. Yes, she was sorry for driving them into a ditch, but she didn't have the opportunity to apologize or explain. The only thing she had time to do was run to the bathroom, and she wasn't even sure she was going to make it.

# 14

Her head was heavy and she was embarrassed. Charly rinsed her hands, then pounded the pushbutton on the wall-mounted electric dryer. It didn't work. She laughed, unsurprised. Every move she'd made since leaving home had proved to be the opposite of what she'd expected. Her phone vibrated in her pocket. Quickly, she dried a hand on her shirt, grabbing the phone. A text from Lola.

My cuzn lives in Detroit. Call her.

She'd sent her cousin's number in a separate text. Charly saved it to her contacts, then exited the bathroom. She smiled when she saw Solomon purchasing medicine at the register. "You okay?" she asked.

Solomon smiled. "I should be asking you the same thing," he teased, opening the bottle of pink liquid, and guzzling it like Outlaw had the liquor. "Let's hope it works 'cause I don't like hospitals."

Charly nodded.

"Here," he said, handing her a bottle of the pink magic potion. "This one's for you."

She drew her brows together in question. "I don't need Pepto. I didn't eat the food."

Solomon laughed. "No, but you took a laxative. Maybe this will stop it from working."

Laxative? What was he talking about? "I didn't take a laxative," Charly said. "The only thing I had was some green tea."

He pointed to a nearby shelf with over-the-counter medications, and Charly saw a bottle of tea exactly like the one she'd bought from the Chinese store. "I think you need to reread it, then compare the ingredients to another laxative."

She was shaking her head when Outlaw walked in. Solomon had been right. Her special green tea was indeed a laxative, a fortified one that contained more laxative medication than the others.

"You ready?" he said to Solomon. "They just pulled the van outta the ditch." He looked at his watch. "And not a second too soon, we got about two hours before the funeral."

Charly noticed he wasn't talking to her, and she hoped he wasn't mad at her. She hadn't meant to drive the van into the ditch. "Outlaw, I'm sorry."

Outlaw looked at her and *tsk*ed. "You sholl is sorry. I don't know what made me let you drive!"

"Alcohol and food poisoning," Solomon reminded. "You can't just leave her here."

Outlaw reared back his head. "And why the heck not? You know how much that tow truck cost . . . ?" He looked at Charly, then pulled a piece of paper from his pocket. "Seventy-five dollars." He eyed her. "You got that, and you can ride to Detroit."

Charly gulped. Yes, she had the money, but if she gave it to Outlaw to cover the towing cost, she knew she wouldn't have enough to get to New York. She wasn't sure how much bus or train fare would cost from Detroit, but whatever the price, she was certain that giving up seventy-five dollars would make her short. "I . . . I . . ."

Solomon looked at her like *Help me help you. Please say the right thing.*

"Don't stutter now. You weren't stuttering when you hopped in the van for a free ride," Outlaw said, scratching his head. "So is you riding or not?" he asked, holding out his hand for the cash.

Charly nodded, then turned her back to them. She reached into her shirt, removed the safety-pinned handkerchief, unfolded it, took out four twenties, and had secured it back in place in seconds. She hated to give up the money, but if she wanted to make the audition in New York, she had to part with it. She handed the cash to Outlaw. "You got change?" she asked.

Outlaw laughed. "Yeah. I can change my mind if you want," he said, pushing the gas station door open and exiting. "I know this big head girl ain't expecting no change, Solomon. Like we don't need five extra dollars in the tank," he complained, walking to the van. "Now y'all get in. I wiped it down, and picked up some number ones from Mickey D's for y'all," he said, pointing to the burger joint that was attached to the building.

Charly, though upset from being eighty dollars short of what she'd had, smiled. Outlaw may complain and curse and drink too much, but he was okay, she decided, biting into the burger he'd bought. His having a meal waiting for her in the van was a clear indication that he'd had no plans of leaving her stranded.

Solomon's grasp was strong, Charly thought, pushing away from him. She'd just hopped out of the van, and was standing on the curb next to her luggage. What he and Outlaw had called Detroit wasn't really Detroit, no more than Belvidere had been the Southside of Chicago, she'd learned. They were actually going to Ann Arbor, Michigan, a town that was about an hour from Motown. "You sure you gonna be cool here?" he asked, stepping back and putting his hands in his pockets.

Charly nodded yes despite not really knowing. She'd called Lola, who in turn texted her cousin, who'd promised to pick up Charly from the University of Michigan, Ann Arbor campus—if Lola, Ms. Cheaper than Everybody, wired money to pay for gas.

"I'll be fine, Solomon. I'll just go in here and grab a brownie and a sandwich," she said, nodding to the Panera Bread behind her. "My ride should be here any second." She looked at her watch. They'd contacted Lola's cousin fifty minutes ago, and Lola had wired the money ten minutes after that. Charly estimated that her ride would be arriving within the next half hour, and she was certain she'd recognize Lola's cousin without problem. According to Lola, she and her cousin had always been mistaken for twins. How many black girls with natural blond hair and blue eyes could there be? Charly wondered.

Solomon licked his lips, then took out his cell phone. He handed it to Charly. "Call yourself. That way you have my number and I have yours. Call me if you need anything." He reached into his pocket, and pulled out some cash. "And take this five. We didn't really need yours for gas. Unc was tripping."

Charly pocketed the five dollars and did as he asked, then waved good-bye to him and Outlaw, who'd stayed in the van pouring himself a little "something-something" as he'd referred to his Big Gulp cup now filled with alcohol.

"You watch yo'self, shorty doowop," Outlaw said, throwing the van in gear as soon as Solomon climbed in the back.

Charly smiled. "Hey, Outlaw!" she yelled. "Just a quick question. How come no one rides in the front?"

Outlaw laughed. "Didn't you see my best friend sitting up here?" he asked. "Sorry if I didn't introduce you. His first name is Jack. Last name is Daniels." He pulled off, and Charly laughed, noticing his license plates for the first time: ALKEE.

She'd ordered and eaten three brownies and a sandwich, and was now on her second cup of coffee. Charly

had called Lola's cousin a million times and had only gotten a message saying the voice mail hadn't been set up.
She'd also texted Lola for the umpteenth time, double
checking the time Lola's cousin was supposed to arrive
and asking for her name. In the midst of all the chaos,
getting Lola's cousin's name had slipped her mind. She
shook her head. Lola still hadn't replied. College students had come and gone, the work shift had changed,
and the second manager of the day had asked her if she
needed anything. Charly looked at her watch. Waiting
for Lola's cousin had proved useless, she decided, getting up from her seat. She wheeled her bags into the
bathroom, then splashed water on her face. A tired feeling had begun to take over again, and she couldn't risk
falling asleep. Sticking her wrists under the faucet, she
waited for the cold stream to help. She'd read somewhere that it gave your body an energy jolt, which is
just what she needed.

The door swung open, and a red-haired girl wearing
glasses and a Panera Bread apron entered with a huge
backpack in her hand. She lifted the bag, setting it on the
counter. It landed with a thud, and Charly could tell it
was heavy. The girl gave Charly a courteous smile as she
stood in the mirror next to her, unzipping the knapsack,
and removing a cell phone and charger. She connected
them and plugged them into an outlet on the wall.

"Excuse me," Charly said, deciding she had to do
something to further her journey. She couldn't just wait
on someone she didn't even know to help her. It didn't
matter if the person she was waiting on was Lola's cousin

or not. Whoever Lola's cousin was, she didn't have allegiance to Charly. "Do you happen to know where the nearest affordable motel or hotel is? I gotta find somewhere to crash before I go."

The girl pressed a button on her phone, then smiled when the cell made music, signaling that it had powered on. She set it down, then took out a tube of gloss from the bag's outside zipper, then pursed her lips in thought. "Well, there's an inn close by, I passed it on my way here. But . . ." She looked at Charly with large, dark brown eyes, opened the tube, and painted her mouth a fantastic gold. "You're kinda young. I'm sure they won't let you stay there." She set down the makeup and took off her apron, revealing the University of Michigan T-shirt she wore underneath.

Charly laughed and shook her head. She waved her hand. "Thanks. I get that all the time, but I'm older than I look. How far is the inn?"

The girl rubbed and pressed her lips together, smoothing out the gloss. She picked up the cell from off the counter and looked at the screen as if she was expecting a call or notification. "Not too far. As a matter of fact, I'm going that way in about five . . . if you want to follow me."

Charly smiled. "Speaking of five, if I give you five dollars, you think you can drop me off? My ride kinda didn't show up."

The girl nodded, then shrugged. "If you don't mind stopping by the store with me first, I don't see why not. I was supposed to be meeting this dude here. But you know how these men are. You try to do right by them, and all they know how to do is do wrong." She stuck out her hand. "I'm Nicole, by the way."

Charly smiled. "I'm Charly."

Nicole shrugged. "I'm so sorry to hear that, but I won't hold it against you. The dude that stood me up, his name is Charles."

# 15

"So where are you going?" Nicole asked as soon as they left through Panera Bread's side exit. She was walking fast, shifting her eyes and anxiously looking around. She'd stopped twice and surveyed the parking lot, and froze every time a car pulled in.

The Charlie guy Nicole had been waiting for must've been very important to her, Charly believed. "A hotel or motel," Charly told her, thinking the girl had to have a short memory.

"We're over here," Nicole said, pointing and then pressing a button on a car key. Lights on a new Jaguar flashed on and off, and the trunk rose.

Charly raised her brows in appreciation of the fine car, and thought it fantastic that someone as young as Nicole drove one. "This is yours? It's nice."

Nicole smiled, then made her way toward the driver's door. She stopped by the rear. "Thanks. Let me take your luggage. I'll just put it in the trunk with the rest of the things." She pointed at Charly's bags.

Charly shook her head. The least she could do was handle her own luggage. The girl was doing her a big enough favor by giving her a ride. She didn't have to play valet too. "That's okay. I got 'em." She wheeled the bags toward the trunk.

Nicole had rounded the car and was in front of Charly, blocking her before she knew it. Charly had no idea the girl could move so fast. "It's no problem really. In fact, I insist. . . . I kinda need to do something mechanical to help get this frustration off my shoulders. I use my mind too much," she explained, reaching for Charly's luggage.

Charly didn't budge. She'd been clipped once already by Grandma Anna, and she wasn't giving someone else the opportunity to steal from her again. She tightened her grip on the extended handle when Nicole put her hands on it. "That's okay. I got it."

Nicole laughed knowingly, her hand still on the handle of Charly's luggage. "I'm not going to steal your stuff, if that's what you're worried about," she told Charly, then extended her left hand to Charly. "You can take the keys if that makes you feel better. I just kinda have something back there I don't want anyone to see. I've had too many people steal from me. You know what I'm saying," she said.

Charly cocked her head sideways. "You don't have drugs or guns or anything like that back there, do you? I mean, you are driving an expensive car for someone your age."

Now it was Nicole's turn to laugh. "I get that all the

time. I'm older than I look too," she deadpanned, staring into Charly's eyes. "But no. I don't have drugs or guns in the trunk. And it's kind of crappy that you'd say that. What, people who look like us can't have nice things? I work hard for my money, Charly."

Charly nodded. She'd been out of order for assuming the worst, and was sure she sounded just like the cops and people who judged others by stereotypes. "Sorry. I just can never be too careful. I've been stolen from a lot too," she explained, taking the car key.

"I can tell," Charly heard Nicole say as she opened the passenger door and got in. Her phone vibrated before she strapped her seat belt around her. Stormy's name popped up on the cell screen.

"Hey!" Charly greeted. "Can you believe Lola's cousin stood me up? I've been here waiting forever. Wait, you do know what I'm talking about, right?" she decided to ask because she wasn't sure her sister knew what was going on. "At this point, Stormy, I'm really considering just coming back home. This whole trip has been terrible."

"Charly. Charly! Stop talking and listen," Stormy demanded.

The trunk closed, and Nicole was on her way to the driver's door. "What is it?" she whispered, not wanting Nicole to know her business. It was bad enough she had just about accused the girl of dealing drugs and transporting guns, she didn't want Nicole to know she was giving a ride to someone who would've been considered a runaway.

"You can't come home, Charly. You didn't pay the cable bill, and Brigette is on a rampage. She said if you ever walk through that door, she's turning you over to juvenile, and I believe her, Charly. The cops were just here and she told them you stole from her. Filed a report and everything."

Charly's heart stopped. Her mother was terrible. "What did you say, Stormy? Did you tell them she's a liar?" She could hear Stormy crying from the other end of the phone. "Don't cry. Please don't." Nicole got in the car and slammed shut the door. Charly held up a finger, signaling that she'd be off the phone in a second.

"I couldn't, Charly," Stormy said, sniffling. "She told me if I said one word, she'd tell the cops that I was in on it, and they'd take me too. She's crazy, Charly. Crazy and coldhearted. I'm leaving too."

Charly exhaled. So she couldn't go back home, but, in her heart, she'd already known that. Deep inside she'd always known she'd never had a home to begin with. "Yes, you are leaving. You are. But I need you to wait. Okay? As soon as I get to New York and get settled, I'm sending for you. I promise."

Stormy was still sniffling. "Are you sure? Because I can't take it here without you."

Charly nodded as if Stormy could see her. "I'm sure. Just let me make and save some money, and I'm sending for you."

Noise could be heard on the opposite end of the line. Brigette's voice blared in the back. "Gotta go. Love you." The line went dead.

Music pumped out of the car speakers, and they hadn't spoken for miles. Charly's thoughts were on saving

Stormy from Brigette. Her mother setting her up to fall over a utility bill didn't surprise her, but her threatening to have Stormy locked up had totally taken her off guard. She didn't want to be rude to Nicole, but she had to get her thoughts together, then her life.

"So . . . New York, huh?" Nicole asked, turning down the volume and hanging a right onto a country road. Rain began pouring from the sky. "I didn't mean to eavesdrop, but it was kinda hard." She turned on the windshield wipers.

Charly glanced at Nicole. "It's okay. It's your car." She shrugged. "I don't know. . . . I gotta make some money."

"Impossible," Nicole said, turning into a shopping center parking lot. She zoomed up and down lanes of cars, looking for a parking spot and swerving around the many potholes.

Charly drew her brows together, thinking about Nicole's comment and wondering why they hadn't parked yet. They'd passed at least a dozen or so empty parking spaces. "There's a spot right there," she said, pointing out the window. "And what do you mean by 'impossible'?"

Nicole shook her head, bypassing the space Charly had pointed to, then drove toward the back of the shopping center and turned onto the alley-looking drive behind the stores. Water splashed as high as an ocean wave on the uneven concrete. "Forgot about the condition of this place when it rains," she said, then mumbled numbers with her mouth, obviously counting. "Eleven," she said to herself, then turned to Charly. "We're here," she said, pulling next to a Dumpster, and putting the car in park. She killed the engine, took off her seat belt, and faced Charly. "Impossible, meaning you can't make money, you have to earn it. And watch out for all the water. It's like miniature rivers around here when it rains."

Now Charly was confused. She reached into her pocket, pulled out the five-dollar bill she was paying Nicole for giving her a ride to the motel, then handed it to her. "Well, I guess you just earned this. Right?"

Nicole snatched the five-dollar bill and laughed. She removed a stack of large bills from her purse and un-folded it. She placed the five inside. "Thanks. I almost forgot about this. But what I said is true. Unless you're a counterfeiter, you can't make it." She pursed her lips, then smacked. "So you need to earn some money, right? Well, if you help me, I may be able to help you."

Charly perked. "I'm listening."

# 16

A small desk with a time clock over it was situated a
few feet from the back entrance. Nicole smiled at
Charly. "You can get to the shopping floor from there,"
she said, pointing down an aisle with hundreds of boxes
on either side. "I'm punching in, then I'll meet you out
front. Look around. We won't be here that long, but,
still, it may be awhile because I have some employees I
gotta check on," she forewarned, making her way toward the desk.

Charly took her time walking down the aisle, wondering what electronic wonders all the boxes held. She was
certain that they contained just about everything a gadget
junkie—namely herself—would love. Pushing through
the swing door that led to the main shopping area, she
half wondered what Nicole was up to, and if she was
going to have to fire any of the employees she had to
check on. The girl had said she'd worked hard to earn

her money, and now Charly knew she hadn't been lying. They'd only left Panera a short time ago, and now Nicole was working again. *A manager*, Charly nodded, impressed.

The mega electronics store was bigger than Charly had imagined, and it was filled with shoppers. Charly perused the aisles, looking at things she couldn't afford. Videos. Music CDs. Televisions. Appliances. The store had everything. Her eyes looked up and to the left. A huge blue sign had the word STEREOS printed in bold yellow. To the right, another display read COMPUTERS. She nodded, deciding to go check out the PCs and Macs she knew would resurrect old angry feelings. She'd almost had a computer just like she'd almost had the new Android. But her mother's stealing had assured she wouldn't have either.

"Can I help you with something?" a young guy asked, as Charly played with a new PowerBook laptop.

"Does this have Wi-Fi?" Charly asked.

The guy reared back his head. "Does it? What computer doesn't nowadays. But this doesn't have just normal Wi-Fi," he began selling, obviously mistaking Charly for a paying customer.

Charly stood and listened and played with the laptop as if she was going to purchase it. She took a quick glance at her watch, and saw that she'd been in the store for over an hour and still hadn't met up with Nicole. She excused herself, telling the guy she'd be right back, then went to look for Nicole. Aisle after aisle, she roamed, and hadn't spotted Nicole anywhere. She was just about to leave out and go look for the Jaguar when the mobile section caught her attention.

"No," she told herself, knowing that if she saw the

phone she'd been saving for, she'd really become angry. But she couldn't help herself. She had to at least touch it.

She'd just picked it up when another employee made his way to her. "I'm just looking," Charly told him before he started trying to sell.

He held up his hands in surrender and wiggled his eyebrows. "I was only going to warn you not to buy this one. A new one's being announced in a couple of days, then released the week after. Some new marketing scheme the company's trying." He winked. "But you know, I'm not supposed to tell you that though."

Charly smiled. The thing the employee had done with his brows reminded her so much of Mason, and made her miss him. She'd only been away from him for a couple of days, but it felt like forever. Now she wondered what he was up to, and thought about Brooklyn.

"So this one's good, but the new one is great. Trust me. It's faster. Has a better camera. And I can't even begin to tell you how fantastic the display is. The images are crystal clear," he rattled.

"And the video camera?" Charly inquired.

"Amazing."

She shook her head and *tsk*ed him. "I guess you're doing presales, huh? What, you're supposed to pretend to give me confidential information about this one, tell me not to buy it because the new one's coming out, and then you're supposed to convince me to prepay for the new one or something? Is that how it goes?" Charly asked, smiling.

The guy shook his head. "We don't do presales. And I could get fired for the information I just gave you. Plus, I don't work off of commission. I just think you're fine and wanted to talk to you," he admitted.

Charly bit her lip, then played with her hair. She tilted her head sideways. "Really? All this because you think I'm fine?"

He nodded. "All this . . . and . . ." He grabbed her hand. "Come with me. I got something to show you."

She only went with him because he was a cutie, she told herself, allowing him to lead her through the mobile section to the counter. He was cute and nice and polite and his brow wiggling reminded her so much of Mason, that's why she'd gone with him. That, and she had nothing else to do while waiting on Nicole.

"Back here," he said, taking her behind the counter. "Look down there. Slide open the drawer, and you'll see." He sidestepped, allowing Charly room. "But don't get up. I can get in trouble if my manager sees you back here."

Charly squatted, then opened the drawer. Her mouth fell open. Sure enough, a newer model of the phone she'd saved for was there. It was sleeker, and lighter, and so, so pretty. "Can I?"

The guy looked around the store, then, without looking down, said, "Go ahead. We're all clear."

Her hands were opening the box, and the phone was in her hand. She powered it on, then scrolled, changing screens with just a swipe of her fingers. Reluctantly, she put it back in the box and set it in the drawer. It made no sense for her to torment herself by playing with a phone she knew she couldn't have, and wouldn't for a long time. All her money and energy would be spent on New

York, getting Stormy there, and making a career for herself. As if saving her from herself, her cell vibrated in her
pocket.

> LOLA: Where r u? My cuzn's been waiting for you
> @ Panera!!!

Charly stood, jetted from behind the counter, and was
on her way to the doors marked EMPLOYEES ONLY without a second thought.

"Hey! You can't go back there," the cute sales guy
with brows like Mason's said, hustling behind her.

Charly veered, looking for the main doors. "I gotta go."

"That way," he said, pointing. "But wait! Here. Take
my card. My cell's on the back. Call me."

Charly nodded, taking his card. "Okay," she said, not
really thinking. Then she caught herself. She couldn't
leave without Nicole. "Can you please page the manager
Nicole for me?"

Sales boy reared back his head. "We don't have a manager named Nicole."

"Are you sure? I just came in with her. She's about my
size, a bit darker-complected, with red hair," she informed him.

Again he said no. "All of our managers are men."

Her heart was in her shoes, and her lungs were on fire
from running full speed around the shopping center to
what she thought was the back entrance to the electronics store. Charly looked around, wondering if she'd
counted wrong. She'd passed eleven doors, counting them
along the way as Nicole had done. But she must've mis-

counted, she told herself. There was no way she could've been right because Nicole's Jaguar was nowhere in sight.

Charly backtracked, then retraced her steps, counting the back entrances to the stores along the way and avoiding the water-filled puddles. She'd walked the pavement two times, starting on one end, then ending on the other. Eleven doors or twelve wouldn't really have mattered, she told herself. The only vehicles behind the shopping center were delivery trucks and semis. A rising heat pushed up and balled in her throat, forming a knot. Her eyes stung from holding back tears. She wanted to cry, to break down, but it wouldn't help. No matter how strong her feelings, nothing could change what she now knew. Nicole had been just like the rest of the thieves in her life. *But why?* she wondered, stepping out of the way of a huge truck speeding toward her. Nicole had a brand-new Jaguar and a lot of money, so Charly couldn't understand the need for her to steal her luggage and leave her stranded.

*Whoosh.* The truck blew by, its tires spitting buckets of water on Charly.

She closed her eyes and stiffened, then let her dam of tears break. She couldn't have been wetter if she were a fish living in the ocean.

# 17

The city bus doors closed behind her, and Charly made her way down the aisle, looking for a place to sit as she held onto each seat, trying to steady herself. Her feet squished inside her boots with each step, and she was sure people were watching her. Rain or storm, she was certain no one could've been more drenched than she.

"I'm telling you, I can't stand these dogs," she heard a woman say as she passed her seat. "If I didn't make so much money from selling 'em, I'd send 'em all to the pound—instead of just this one. Well, actually, I ain't sending it to the pound. Too much paperwork. I'm gonna leave it in a box somewhere," the woman declared.

"Why don't you just drop it off at a vet? Don't just leave the thing to die," some other passenger said.

Charly released her wet weight in the seat just in front of the bus's back doors and put her purse on the empty one next to her. She scrunched her face at the squishy feeling of her wet pants sticking to the plastic seat. The driver assured her that the Panera Bread was on the bus's route, and promised to let her know when the stop was coming up. Charly only hoped they were talking about the same restaurant. Her recent travel history dictated that there would be some sort of problem, and that's what she was expecting.

"I'm going to Wally World," the loud lady up front was still talking. "I'm gonna sell as many of 'em as I can. Some man 'posed to meet me there to buy the litter, but he don't want no runts," she was telling someone in the seat across from her, who Charly couldn't hear.

For less than a second, Charly wondered what a runt was; then the woman answered her question. She held up the cutest dog Charly had ever seen, gripping it by the loose skin on the back of its neck. Charly winced, sure that the way the woman was handling the dog had to hurt. Thoughts of Brooklyn and her sad eyes made Charly's heart bleed for the puppy.

"You know pets aren't allowed on the bus," the driver announced over the bus's speakers through a CB-like device.

The lady laughed, then removed the dog from sight. "I know the rules. You know that," the lady said loudly. "And you know these ain't no pets. These here dogs are my job—how I make money. So I guess you can call 'em commercial property." She laughed, reaching across the aisle and slapping someone five. "All except that one," she continued. "That one gon' be the property of puppy heaven. See what I'm saying? Put. To. Sleep. Rat poisoning or something should do."

Charly cringed and stared straight ahead. The poor puppy had no more of a chance at happiness or living than she'd had at Brigette's house.

"About thirty minutes to Panera," the driver announced, glancing at Charly in the large rearview mirror.

Charly nodded and smiled a thank-you. Warm air blew from the vents above, and Charly settled in for the ride. Her eyes were tired, and she decided to close them for a moment. A quick nap would let her rest up and make the ride go by faster.

"Panera in two stops," she thought she heard the driver say as someone pulled her boot. Her eyes shot open. She'd been through a lot, but to think someone would have the nerve to take her boots while she was still in them was a bit much. She moved her feet around on the floor, and didn't feel anything. She had to have been dreaming, she told herself, closing her lids again.

"Ouch!" A sharp pain punctured her leg, and she reached for the wound, opening her eyes again and looking around. There was no one around, but she was almost certain she'd been stabbed with a needle. Her eyes moved to the seat next to her. Her purse was gone. Gone. Charly jumped up, frantically looked around; then she calmed. Her bag had slid on the floor. Relief moved through her as she sat back down in the seat and reached for the long strap. She froze. The purse moved. She didn't know whether to scream or run. She opened her mouth to yell out, but was silenced by a slight whimper.

"Next stop, Panera" the bus driver said, nodding to Charly.

"Puppy. Puppy. Puppy!" Puppy Peddler called. "The

runt done got away. She gotta be somewhere 'round here. Soon as I find her, I'm throwing her into the water. Never mind all this poisoning stuff," she said. "I almost forgot about that . . . Drowning always works."

Charly opened her purse all the way and locked eyes with the runt the lady was looking for. The bus pulled over, and a loud, airy noise sounded as the doors opened.

"Panera!" the driver informed Charly.

Charly looked over and saw that she had indeed been taken to the correct location. She breathed deeply, pushed the puppy down into her purse, then exited the bus, ignoring Puppy Peddler's pleas for someone to help her locate the dog that she was planning to drown.

The rain had stopped. Charly walked quickly toward the Panera Bread, looking for someone who resembled Lola. As if sensing her name being thought of, Lola's name popped up on Charly's cell phone screen.

"I'm here," Charly said instead of hello.

"Whew. Good. I'm glad to hear it, and it's about time. You should've seen all I had to go through to get that money to you. First off, you know I didn't have it. Secondly, I had to go to Smax, who made me give up a month's worth of free meals for it. Now you know you owe me for that. You know I don't give up my meals, Charly," Lola said. "I guess Stormy told you about Brigette, huh?" she rattled.

Charly nodded her head, listening to Lola go on and on, all while looking for Lola's cousin. Pressing her forehead against one of Panera Bread's huge windows, she didn't see anyone inside who resembled Lola. Stepping back, she looked over and saw a bench. She could wait there, she decided, then saw it was wet. She'd had enough water on her butt, and didn't feel like enduring her pants sticking to her any more than they already were. A dog barked somewhere in the distance, catching Charly's attention. A huge sign for a pet store that she hadn't before noticed suddenly stood out. Her cash was extremely low, but her new dog would need food. She shrugged. Lola had wired money to her cousin to give to Charly.

"Why not?" Charly said to herself, walking toward the pet store.

"Why not what?" Lola asked from the other end of the phone.

"Oh, I was . . ." Charly's world stopped spinning. Just up ahead, a Jaguar just like Nicole's was parked alongside the curb. The trunk and driver's side door was open, but Charly couldn't see the owner.

"Hold on," Lola said, then clicked over.

Charly sped up, petting the dog, who'd stuck out its head from her purse. She narrowed her eyes, trying to see who the car belonged to.

"You there? Charly?" Lola asked. "Dang, I hate these three-ways. I can never figure out how to conference these dumb calls."

"I'm here. Can you hear me?" Charly asked, still walking. The car was farther than she'd thought.

"Yes. Can you hear us? My cousin's on the line."

A garbled, mechanical noise met Charly's ears. Obviously, someone was on the phone with Lola. Charly just couldn't hear them. "I can only hear you, Lola. It must be a bad connection."

"I can hear both of you guys fine," Lola said. "She said

she's already there, Charly. In the parking lot waiting for you. She said she needs you to hurry up because she left her friend at the store to come get you."

Charly stopped walking and looked around. There was no one in front of Panera Bread, and she didn't see anyone or anything except the Jaguar that looked a lot like Nicole's. She shook her head, ready to fight. If she ever laid eyes on Nicole again, only God and the angels would be able to help her, she promised herself. She was tired of people stealing from her, and she swore that Nicole would have to take a beat-down for all of them. She was only feet from the car now, and was almost sure it was the same Jag.

"What's your cousin's name?" she finally asked Lola. Then her eyes bulged. She could see inside the open trunk, and, sure enough, lavender luggage was inside.

"Her name's Nicole. She said she's driving a new Jaguar. You can't miss her. We look just alike," Lola said enthusiastically.

Charly's jaw dropped and her feet froze. A young lady about her size and a little bit darker-complected appeared from the front of the car, and closed the trunk. Her hair was so blond it was almost white, and it was all over her head just like Lola's.

She turned and locked eyes with Charly. "Charly?" she laughed. "I can't believe it's you."

Charly just looked. She was face-to-face with the same Nicole she'd been with for hours. The same Nicole she thought had stolen from her and left her stranded. "What happened to your hair and glasses?" Charly asked. "Why'd you leave me?"

Nicole waved her hand, walking up to Charly. "Oh, I change my looks all the time. Wigs. Contact lenses. Glasses. You name it, I rock it." She smiled. "I left because I was supposed to come get *you* from here. . . ." She shrugged. "Lola finally got through to me while I was in the store, and said it was an emergency. As you know, my phone had died. Remember, I was charging it before we left." She laughed, shaking her head. "I can't believe all that time I thought I was waiting for a dude named Charlie, I was waiting for you. Stupid text on the cells. I don't know why they call the auto-correct feature smart text." She pulled out her phone, pressed a couple of buttons and showed it to Charly. "See?"

Charly shook her head and laughed. Lola's first text read:

Charlie @ Panera, Plymouth Rd.

"Okay. You really had phone problems. Auto-correct smart text and dead battery. I tried calling you, but kept getting sent to your voice mail that hasn't been set up, by the way."

"Let's go," Nicole said. "We gotta get you to New York."

# 18

Downtown Detroit was live. L.I.V.E. and in living color. Girls and women had flawless and sometimes colorful hairdos. A lot of older men resembled males from an era when they wore suits that matched from the lining all the way down to the socks and insides of Dobb brims. Many were in different flavors, and looked like they had been designed by Crayola. The younger guys stood out like they were fluorescent. The dudes weren't bright. They just seemed extra gorgeous, and Charly couldn't help but look at them. Still, though, on West Jefferson, none were as beautiful as Mason.

"Haa-shew!" Nicole sneezed for the kazillionth time, then rubbed her eyes. "If I didn't grow up around animals, I'd think I was allergic to your dog. I must be coming down with something," she said, turning down a street lined with apartment buildings, shotgun houses, and brownstones.

Charly covered her mouth and nose. The last thing she needed was to catch a cold. The dog wiggled on her lap, licking her wrist. She smiled.

"I still can't believe that lady was gonna put that tiny thing to sleep," Nicole said, nodding toward the puppy. "So you thought of a name yet?" she asked.

Charly held up the dog and looked into its eyes. She'd been eyeing him on her lap for the better part of the trip, and couldn't think of a name for him. Her eyes moved from his cute little puppy face to his stomach to his tail. Something was missing. "Um . . . well, it won't be a boy's name," she told Nicole. "It seems that he is a she."

Nicole laughed. "We're terrible dog owners. We've been calling *her* a *him* for almost an hour. We're here," she announced, pulling into an apartment building parking lot.

They got out of the Jaguar, and made their way to the back of the car. Charly put the dog on the ground and tightly gripped the leash they'd stopped and purchased from the pet store along with food, a toy, a collar, and an inexpensive dog tag that had Marlow's name and Charly's number engraved on it. She was waiting for Nicole to open the trunk, then remembered that Nicole didn't want her to see the contents. She began to walk away.

"I know you don't expect me to get my stuff *and* yours too," Nicole said.

Charly raised her brows. "You didn't want me to see what was in it before—"

"Before I knew you were Lola's best friend. That changes everything." She put her hands on her hips and deadpanned. "So, best friend, I suggest you come help me. We are almost related, after all." She popped the trunk and took out a folded shopping cart.

"What in the . . . H-E-Double-L?" Charly asked, disbelief on her face. The trunk of Nicole's car had enough expensive merchandise to fund a small village. Mink and leather coats. Jewelry. Designer handbags. Shoes that retailed for almost a thousand dollars in magazines. Charly's eyes lit. *Electronics.* "Oh my . . ." she said, picking up a box as if it would break. "This is the phone the guy in the store showed me. This hasn't even been released yet. How did you . . . ?"

Nicole unfolded the shopping cart, laughing and ignoring Charly's question. She took out Charly's luggage set, and handed it to her. "Can't believe this trunk is so deep. Who would think all this would fit in here?" she said, filling the cart. "Let's go," she said, then closed the trunk and pressed a button. The car alarm beeped, signaling it was activated.

What Charly assumed to be Nicole's apartment building wasn't really her residence at all. "This way," Nicole had instructed, wheeling the shopping cart toward the back of the parking lot, then pushing it to the side. "Help me," she said to Charly, then walked behind a huge Dumpster. Charly raised her brows, then rolled her luggage next to Nicole's things. She wrapped the dog's leash on the telescopic handle of her bag so the nameless puppy couldn't run away and followed Nicole.

"Here," Nicole said, handing a wooden crate to Charly, and then another and another. With the crates out of the way, Charly saw a steel door that had wheels on the bottom. Nicole pressed a couple of buttons on a keypad, and

Charly could hear a faint click. With two hands and a bit of woman power, Nicole slid open the door until it all but disappeared behind tall, overgrown and unkempt bushes. "Go ahead and go in," Nicole instructed, stepping to the side and rearranging the wooden crates, stacking them next to the opening.

Charly got her luggage and scooped up the puppy, then entered through the opening. Her eyes strained in the darkness, trying to see where she was. Suddenly, low lighting alongside a stacked-stone walkway turned on automatically, allowing her to see clearly. The yard resembled a semi-fortress, boxed in by steel gates that were higher than she was tall. There were pine trees around the perimeter of the small space, which looked like an English garden.

"Year-round greenery. They don't shed," Nicole explained as if her backyard being fortress-like was normal. She slid the gate door until it clicked.

Charly stepped off the walkway to allow Nicole room to go around her and lead the way. Her eyes brightened more and more. She was in disbelief, and had never seen such a yard before. Her eyes landed on the back of the brownstone, and she looked for signs of life in the windows. Surely, Nicole couldn't live in the big space alone. There had to be other tenants, she thought.

"Come in," Nicole said, unlocking the back door and entering. The lights popped on.

Charly stood by the door, gazing inside. Hard flooring that looked as if it belonged in a five-star hotel was underneath expensive furniture. Statues and paintings decorated what must've been a den. "Marble?" she asked.

Nicole nodded and shrugged. "Yeah. A donation," she explained. "Come in. Don't just stand there."

Hesitantly, as if she would break anything she touched, Charly eased inside. Everything about Nicole had the wow factor. Charly was afraid to wheel her luggage across such an expensive floor, and even more afraid of putting the dog down on it. If either she or the dog destroyed anything in Nicole's place, she knew she'd never be able to replace or fix it.

Nicole waved her hand in a follow-me motion, then journeyed into another area of the house. "You can sleep here," she said, pointing to a sofa in a small office space, which was really a hallway. Bookshelves with a recessed desk were on one wall, the couch was on the opposite one, facing the workstation. "You can get to the bathroom through there." She pointed left. "Kitchen's over here."

Charly looked left and right, taking note. "Where's your bedroom?" she asked, thinking it had to be on another floor. The brownstone was large, and what Nicole had shown her of the place was small.

"We passed it. It's right off the living room where we came in." She ran her fingers through her wild blond hair, then rubbed her eyes. She sneezed. "Mmm. I need to take some medicine, maybe some vitamins. I don't know where this cold is coming from, and my eyes itch."

Charly put her luggage next to the sofa. She cradled the puppy to her, then bounced it gently as if it were a baby. "I don't understand. The place looks so huge from the outside. And I don't know why, but I assumed you lived in the whole building."

Nicole laughed. "I guess Lola doesn't know. If she did, I'm sure you would because she can't hold water. But I do own the whole building, and I'm the only one who lives here."

Charly sat, still cradling the puppy. "How old are you?" she had to ask. Nicole looked way too young to have so much, and she wondered what she really had and how she'd gotten it. After all, Lola had had to wire money for Nicole to come get her.

"Twenty-two."

Charly's eyes bulged. She held up the dog to her face and began rubbing noses with her. She didn't know what else to say to Nicole without seeming so nosy, so she stayed quiet.

"Question," Nicole said, walking in front of Charly and squatting. She petted the puppy from behind. "You've never had an animal before or something? You seem very attached. Too attached not to have named this dog yet."

Charly thought back to the dog her dad had surprised her with when she was four. The same one her mother had dropped off at the pound less than twenty-four hours later. She nodded. "Yes, for a hot second. Then Brigette—that's my mother, unfortunately—took Marlow away when I was at daycare." A saddened smile crossed her face as she thought about Marlow.

Nicole patted the puppy's head. "Now you have another Marlow, and your mom can't take her."

Charly smiled. Yes, she did have another Marlow. "That's her name. In memory of my first puppy, this one's named Marlow 2, like in the number two." She stopped petting Marlow 2, then looked Nicole dead in her eyes.

"Okay, so now that I'm here, I think I should know. What do you do, Nicole?"

"I'm a contractor. You know, like real estate? Building?"

Charly was impressed. She'd never met a contractor before, though she'd seen several on HGTV and knew a bit about what they did. "Cool. So you help build houses, apartments? What?"

Nicole stood and winked. She waved her hand for Charly to follow her. "I build people and communities. And so will you . . . if you want to make money to get to New York." She shrugged. "Then there's always the row," she said, laughing and confusing Charly because she had no idea what a row was.

# 19

Nicole's brownstone was a warehouse of goods. What she'd taken out of the car trunk couldn't put a dent in what was before Charly. They stood in the front of the house on the bottom floor, and shelves that extended to the ceiling were stocked with imperishable groceries. Canned goods, cereal, bags of rice and oats, condiments, and any food items with extended shelf life that Charly could think of were there. Around the perimeter of the room, stand-up freezers, the kind that major supermarkets had, were stocked. Some stuff was frozen, other things like eggs, milk, cheese, and quick mixes of hash browns and microwavable entrees filled them.

"I don't follow," Charly said.

"You will," Nicole assured, walking toward a staircase, then climbing it.

On the other floor were housewares. From living room

sets to bedroom suites to breakfast tables and mattresses to towels and rugs, Nicole had them all. On the third level, Charly discovered, were clothes and shoes on one side, and electronics on the other. She shook her head, sure that Nicole was just a higher-level thief. What else could explain all the goods?

"Okay, so here's how it goes." She leaned against a table with a bunch of electronics on top, folded her arms, then deadpanned Charly. "I'm sorta like Robin Hood."

"You steal from the rich and give to the poor." Charly eyed her.

Nicole shook her head, laughing hysterically. She sneezed. "No. I'm no thief. At least not in the literal legal sense of the word, but I do get away like a thief in the night. I do what I do, get in and get out, and they never see me coming or going."

Charly nodded. That was all she could do. Nod and try to figure out if she should run or not.

"Today, for example. When you saw me in Panera . . . well, I don't work there, I just had to look like I did. I know someone who knows someone who knows someone else—that's always the first key to getting in. Knowing someone. Well, restaurants like Panera—not necessarily Panera per se . . . that's the second key—you *never* give your resources. Anyway, many restaurants and fast-food joints throw their food out at the end of the day. There's no recycling unless I recycle." She shifted, eyeing Charly. "I take what they're throwing out and I give it to families, the community. Churches, shelters . . . you get it."

Charly nodded again. That made sense, but it didn't

cover enough. "The groceries, clothing . . . electronics? I mean, the phone you just took out of the trunk hasn't even been released yet."

Nicole shrugged. "Same difference. Some grocery stores, mostly the ones in affluent neighborhoods, discard food when it reaches the expiration date or right before. *But!*" She held up her index finger. "The food is still good according to government standards. The clothes have inconsistencies . . . could be a label was sewn in upside down, same with shoes, mattresses, et cetera, et cetera. Now the electronics . . . that one is a hard one. But I'm sure you've heard of scratch and dent."

Charly cuddled Marlow 2. "Not that phone. That phone's not even out yet. Trust me, I know. It was because of the model that's on the market now that I left Illinois. Brigette—my mother—stole the money I was saving to buy it. She did the same with my computer money, mountain bike savings—you name it, she took it."

Nicole turned around, shifted through the items on the table, then turned to face Charly. She threw a box in the air, and Charly caught it with one hand. "Take it. It's yours."

Charly's eyes bulged. In her hand she held an even newer edition of the Android she'd been saving months for. "I . . . uh . . . I don't know what to say."

"Thank you is good enough. And, just so you know, even things that haven't hit the market are thrown out too. Most stores just report the problem to the manufacturer, input a few things in the computer system, then toss the stuff. I think it's a write-off on both ends. Something like that. No one loses." Nicole walked up to

Charly. She sneezed again. "So you want to make some money to get to New York or not?"

Charly shrugged. "Two other questions first. If you give all this stuff away, how can you afford such a nice place and expensive car? And if Lola wired you money for me, why haven't you given it to me?"

"Nice," Nicole said, nodding. "You're quick. And quick equals merchandise. One, everything I have has been donated to me—mostly anonymously—because of what I do. I've been doing this since I was seventeen, and I've helped a lot of people. Some grew up, made a lot of money, and donate whenever. Some died, and willed me things or cash. Two, Lola wired money for me to come get you. I told her I couldn't just take off work, and she said she'd compensate me for the whole day. So," Nicole said, shrugging, "technically, it's not your money. But if it makes you feel better, we used it on gas and dog stuff for Marlow 2." Nicole sneezed again, and tears streaked down her face. Her eyes were reddening.

The sun shone a brilliant orange, warming Charly and Marlow 2 as they walked down the block. Marlow's tail wagged and her feet pitter-pattered, taking tiny steps as Charly guided her toward the grass to relieve the dog's bladder. Today, they'd taken a different route, but every day Charly had been sure to walk Marlow so the puppy would be properly house-trained. Marlow sniffed, walked in circles, changed her mind, then squatted, and then changed her mind again. She was doing what Charly referred to as the pre-potty dance that Marlow did for what seemed like minutes before finally lightening her bladder. Charly nodded, knowing Marlow was just getting started, and took the time to glance around the low-income neighborhood where they were. It reminded her of home. Not the houses, but the feeling of familiarity. The way the people waved and spoke to one another, it seemed as if everyone knew everyone, and that made her miss her sister and Smax and the crew. Charly smiled, looking at Marlow and thinking how much Stormy would love the puppy. Unlike Mason's dog, Brooklyn, Marlow had no problem being on a leash, except for the occasional unsuccessful dash she tried to make into the street. As small as she was, she seemed to think that passing cars were her toys, and she wanted to play with all of them. People too, Charly noticed, when Marlow ran toward a group of teens sitting on the porch of a dilapidated house.

"Marlow," Charly called, taking her cell from her pocket and scrolling to Stormy's number. She pressed TALK, then held the phone to her ear while watching Marlow and waiting for Stormy to answer.

"Hey, puppy," one of the neighborhood girls greeted Marlow.

Charly smiled and tugged lightly on Marlow's leash. She didn't want to seem rude, but she had things to do. Namely, go to the corner store and get a list of people in need of food who'd tried to purchase things on credit. Charly shook her head. She'd grown up around people who'd used old-school paper food stamps to buy things other than food, and had even seen her mom buy someone's EBT card for half of the credit that was on it. Still, she had a hard time believing that corner stores issued credit. She shrugged. If that's what Nicole said, then it must've been true. Maybe things were done differently in Detroit. "Come on, Marlow," Charly said, and disconnected the call. Stormy hadn't answered, but Charly had left a message.

Marlow stood her ground, then began yapping at the teens. Her tail stiffened and stood straight up. Charly reared back her head. She'd never seen Marlow so aggressive, but knew she couldn't do anyone harm. Marlow was tiny.

A girl stood, cradling a puppy in her arm. "She must smell my dog," she said, walking down the creaking porch stairs and over to Charly. Her hair blew in the breeze. "Is that a Maltese?"

Charly took a good look at Marlow. She really had no idea what was Marlow's breed. She shrugged, and her phone vibrated. "One sec," she said to the girl, then took the call. "Stormy," Charly said, turning her back on the girls. She smiled, breathing a bit easier. She'd missed her sister more than she'd thought, and took only seconds to update her about her life. She was in Detroit. She was safe. She was going to New York as soon as she helped the homeless. She told Stormy all she could think of before hanging up to allow Stormy time to study. "Yes, Stormy. I'm great. I promise. Talk soon." She hung up, turning back to the girls, who were obviously in her conversation.

"So, is it? A Maltese?" the girl repeated.

Charly looked at Marlow, then shrugged again. "I'm not sure."

Another girl, a bit older, was standing in the doorway

wearing an obviously dirty headscarf. She laughed. "Sounds like you and Petey, Pee-Wee. You don't know what y'all is either."

The girl holding the dog laughed, completely unfazed by the other girl's rude remark. "I know, right?" She set down her dog on the ground in front of Marlow. With a loose rope tied around his neck, he walked straight to Marlow's butt and began sniffing. "Think your dog and Petey can play? He's too little to play with the other dogs 'round here. All they seem to get 'round here are rotties and pits."

Charly only nodded. Normally—weeks ago—she would've been more friendly, but any automatic friendliness she'd previously had had been replaced by an automatic distrust. People stealing from you could do that. Could make you not trust a soul until they earned it, that's what Nicole had said.

"What? You deaf or something?" the girl standing in the doorway asked, eyeing Charly like she didn't care for her. "Or you just think you too cute to talk to us 'cause you light with long hair?"

Charly's eyes shifted. She wasn't in her territory, and thought it better for her not to say anything. She was in a rough neighborhood, and didn't know if the girl had a weapon or not. Plus, she didn't know how many people were in the house.

"Oh, so you are deaf!" the girl repeated, scratching her head and making her dirty scarf shift. "Probably a punk too."

Suddenly Petey darted toward the street, his loose rope hanging in his owner's hand. Off his makeshift leash, he was headed straight for a car cruising down the block blasting music. Without hesitation, Charly scooped up Marlow, then darted after Petey. She stood in the middle of the road, holding Marlow in one arm, and extending her open palm to the car like a crossing guard stopping traffic.

"What the . . . ?" the driver yelled out of the window, screeching to a stop. "You crazy or something?" he continued, throwing in a few expletives, mostly curses that began with the letters B and F.

Charly picked up Petey, who'd made his way to her side. "Sorry," she said to the angry driver.

"Thank you so much," Pee-Wee said, meeting Charly as she made her way back to the sidewalk, then relieved her of Petey. "I don't know what I would do if something happened to him. I ain't never had a mother or father." She shrugged. "I don't even know what I'm mixed with. So he's all I got."

Charly nodded. She understood more than Pee-Wee knew. "No problem."

"This is a safe house," Pee-Wee explained. "For girls like me. I don't have a family and the system can't find room for me in foster care. No one wants to foster a fifteen-year-old." Her eyes dropped to the ground with her admittance.

Charly smiled, her face contradicting her feelings. She wasn't happy about Pee-Wee's situation. She was glad that she may've found someone for her and Nicole to help. That was the business they were in—helping those in need. "Here. Take this," she said to Pee-Wee, unclasping Marlow's collar and still attached leash. "They're about the same size, so it should hold him and keep him safe."

Now Ms. Dirty Headscarf was all the way on the porch, with a hand on her hip and dirt on the bottoms of her bare feet. "Oh. So now you can talk, huh?" She snaked her neck. "What, you think you somebody 'cause you saved that dumb little dog and gave Pee-Wee here some sloppy seconds? You think you can just walk down *my* block and ain't nothing gone happen to you? I'll stomp you and that little runt you walking. Ain't that right, Pee-Wee?"

Charly's eyes shot to Pee-Wee's in question, and the girl looked to the ground, obviously scared. She handed Marlow to Pee-Wee, then pulled her hair back. In three moves, she'd wrapped it in a tight bun. She stepped up and cleared her throat. She'd had enough of Ms. Dirty Headscarf.

"Let's be clear," Charly said, throwing daggers with her eyes. "You don't know me and, trust to know, you don't want to." She shook her head, then bit her bottom lip. "And you're not stomping nothing around here but your feet on the ground. You put no fear in my heart. Now if you wanna do this, we can do this." She held out her arms. "Space and opportunity."

The girls eyes widened, but they weren't looking at Charly. They were directed at something behind her. "Oh . . ." the girl in the dirty scarf said in defeat.

Charly looked over her shoulder. Nicole was in the middle of the street, the Jaguar idled, and Nicole's hand out the window. In it was a purple bag. "You good,

Charly?" Nicole asked, swinging the sack in small circles, something inside jingling.

Charly darted her eyes to Nicole, then back to the girl she'd exchanged words with. "I'm straight. Just trying to help out my new friend, Pee-Wee."

Pee-Wee smiled.

Nicole nodded, still swinging the bag in her hand. "Okay. Cool. Let's roll."

Charly shook her head. From what she and Nicole had talked about, she'd have to venture this way again. There were a few elderly people on the block who needed them—people that Charly was supposed to help so she could earn some bucks to make it to New York—and it was the fastest route to the stores. She waved her hand at Nicole. "Go ahead. I'm good." She looked at Ms. Dirty Headscarf. "I'm from the South Side—where they don't do drive-bys, they raise us to do walk-bys. We ain't gonna have no more problems. I'll meet you at the house."

Pee-Wee looked at the girl with the dirty headscarf. "You done messed up now. She with Nicole, and you know what that means."

The older girl jetted in the house with her head hanging. Charly took it all in. Nicole with a purple bag, Pee-Wee's attitude changing and becoming more sure, and Ms. Dirty Headscarf running like a coward. It seemed Nicole was a lot more than a temporary roommate and community do-gooder. Charly just didn't know what that more was. Yet.

# 20

A sneeze awoke Charly from her sleep. With a rush, she sat up. This time the sound didn't come from Nicole, it came from Marlow. Charly felt Marlow to see if she had a fever; then she caught herself. How was she to know if a dog had a fever or not? Gently, she shook Marlow, but barely got a response. Worry moved through her. Just earlier Marlow had been running and jumping through the house and yard as if she were in the circus. "You okay?"

Marlow still didn't move. Charly picked her up, and her head just collapsed in Charly's hand. "Nicole!" Charly yelled. "Nicole! Get up!"

"What is it?" Nicole said, rubbing her eyes and sneezing in the doorway.

"I think Marlow's dying. Look," she said, barely tapping Marlow's head and making it roll. "See, she can't even hold it up. She's listless. . . . I think that's what they call it."

Nicole yawned; then her body jerked with another sneeze. "Take the car."

Charly set Marlow on the sofa, grabbed a pair of pants out of the suitcase, and pulled them on. She tucked in her nightgown, then fastened them. She stepped in her brown combat boots, not even thinking of lacing the red shoestrings. "No. I don't know where the vet is, and I've only driven once in my life. I crashed then."

The twenty-four-hour veterinarian clinic was a madhouse. A three-legged dog bumbled by, trying to escape its owner and veterinary assistants. A cat sat in a big open box, crying out, giving birth. And a parrot, perched on its owner's shoulder, extended huge wings, then relieved itself on the floor.

"Oh!" Nicole yelled, then sneezed loudly. Her shoulders hunched and her eyes turned color-crayon red.

"You okay?" Charly asked, then turned to the receptionist and explained what was happening with Marlow.

"Oh!" Nicole said again with a garbled voice. Her tone was low and Charly could barely make out what she was saying.

Nicole clasped her hands around her throat, then took one and pounded on her chest. She was trying to say something.

"What?" Charly asked, still holding a limp Marlow.

"Outside. Outside!" the receptionist yelled. "Take her outside. She can't breathe! There's a lady out here who can't breathe!" she shouted toward the back.

Charly's heart dropped. She had no idea what to do. Nicole couldn't breathe and Marlow wasn't fully conscious. Turning her face from side to side, she looked for help, but everyone was too busy with animal problems of their own.

"Here! Give her here!" the receptionist demanded, reaching for Marlow.

Charly handed the receptionist Marlow, then thought of something. She reached into her pocket, pulled out a wad of money. "Take this too. I don't know how much it is, but it should be enough to start," she said, then rushed over to Nicole.

"I got her. I got her," she said, referring to Marlow. "I'll take her in the back. Go help your friend. She's losing color. I'm sending someone to help."

Nicole was bent over just outside the door, wheezing and trying to pound herself on the back when Charly got to her. Balling her fist, she banged on Nicole's back like she'd seen people do in the movies when someone had food caught in their throats.

"Here," a veterinary worker said, then stuck Nicole in the arm with something that looked like an ink pen. "It's for allergic reactions."

Nicole wheezed with her chest heaving. Then she leaned against the brick wall and slid to the ground. She breathed for a couple of minutes that seemed to take a small eternity. Her color began to return. "Ahh," she finally uttered.

The vet worker nodded. "I knew it. She's allergic to animals. Very," he said to Charly, then turned to Nicole. "I advise you to stay away from anything that has fur. The only reason that you haven't had a reaction until now is because her dog," he said, looking at Charly, "has hair. Not fur. Still though, dander."

"No fur? Not even mink coats?" she asked, and Charly knew Nicole was almost back to her normal self.

She looked at her new friend, happy to see her better. Then something hit her hard. Another problem. How was she going to bunk with Nicole long enough to make money to get to New York if Nicole was allergic to Marlow? For the first time in a long time, Charly closed her eyes. If there was a God in heaven, there had to be a way. She couldn't get rid of Marlow. Wouldn't. "I need help. . . ." she called on the universe, and knew that it would assist her.

Nicole sat up straight, then pushed herself to her feet. "What kind of dog is it?" she asked, looking at the veterinarian employee, who was making his way back inside the twenty-four-hour clinic.

He held the door open with one hand. "Huh?"

Nicole crossed her arms. "I asked what kind of dog we brought in. You must know since you said its got hair, not fur. It's about yea small," she said, holding her hands about eight inches apart. "Caramel and white. Female."

The worker looked to the sky as if his answer was in

the stars. "If you're talking about that puppy, the beautiful one who probably literally ran her sugar level low because she's so small, and really only needed a tablespoon of honey to raise her glucose, it's a shih tzu." He eyed Nicole.

"How much is she worth?" Nicole asked.

Charly stood silent for a second. She watched in horror as Nicole turned from caring friend who wanted to help her make money to get to New York to a puppy peddler. "No," she finally said. "Marlow's not for sale."

The vet worker smiled at Charly. "Good for you. Really good."

Nicole put her hands on her hips, then pivoted her head toward Charly. "Think about what you're saying, Charly. You need a place to stay. You need me to help you get to New York." She turned to the veterinarian employee again. "Well? How much?"

He laughed, shaking his head. "Not that it's gonna really matter, 'cause your friend here, the owner, doesn't seem the least bit interested in selling. But since you really want to know . . ." He held a finger up to his mouth in thought. "If she's purebred, and I can almost tell you for certain that she is because I'm an ethical breeder who's listed with the American Kennel Club, for her size and sex, she'd easily sell for a thousand upward. She's a little small, but nowadays, people pay more for the runts . . . if they're marketed as teacups."

Nicole gave Charly a hard look, then turned toward her car, which was parked at the clinic's entrance. Charly shook her head, following after Nicole. She

knew what direction Nicole was headed with her questioning, and she wasn't willing to take it there with her.
She wasn't getting rid of Marlow. "Nicole?" she called
as Nicole slipped into the driver's seat. "Can I talk to
you?"

"A thousand dollars? For a dog?" Nicole asked the vet
worker, an incredulous look on her face. She turned to
Charly. "Charly, you better sell her. If it was me, I'd sell
her," she stated matter-of-factly. "Did you hear that? A
stack for a dog," she said, using the street term for a
thousand dollars.

Charly shook her head, then put her palm on Nicole's
arm to get her attention. "I don't want to do it, Nicole. I
know it's a lot of money, but—"

"But nothing." She shrugged. "It's simple. I'm allergic.
Sell her." Nicole's hand was on her hip and her stare was
stabbing holes in Charly's plan to keep Marlow. "End of
discussion."

Charly's brows rose. End of discussion, her pinkie toe.
Nicole could help her and had, but that didn't give her
the right to be a dictator. "Nicole, you're not being fair.
Lola wouldn't—"

Nicole held up her hand, stopping Charly midsentence.
"Listen, Charly, I know you and my family are super
close, but, here in the D, we don't rock like that. Here it's
every man—or woman—for herself. It's about dollars
and sense." She pointed to her temple. "If it don't make
money, it don't make sense. And it don't make sense if it
don't make money. And, right now, you or Marlow ain't
making either." Nicole shut the driver's side door and

started her Jaguar. Her expression said a decision needed to be made.

Charly didn't want to move out of Nicole's fabulous brownstone, but had to. Nicole was allergic to Marlow, and there was no getting around that because Nicole wasn't going to take medication to tolerate someone else's animal. And Charly didn't think her unreasonable for not doing so. Just as she saw nothing wrong with her refusing to get rid of Marlow. Point blank. Period. So there was no getting around that either. She loved her dog, and would give her a loving home once she found one, and she'd make sure that the warmth of hers rivaled the coldness that Brigette's house offered.

"Okay, then. Keep the dog. I'll be right back with your stuff," Nicole said, pulling out of the parking lot. And just that quick, Charly was on her own again.

When Nicole returned an hour later with Charly's bags, she still hadn't figured out her next move.

"You're going to be okay," Nicole stated, hanging partially out of the driver's seat window. It wasn't a question. It was a demand.

Charly wheeled her luggage to the side of the car, then up on the curb. "Thanks for helping me out," she said, not knowing what else she should say. She'd thought of her and Nicole as friends, but Nicole's nasty blowup had proved otherwise. Nicole had said for her it was only about money. Everything else was secondary. Family and friendships included, she had admitted to Charly once she knew Charly wouldn't be of use to her "building people and the community" business, which only served as a distraction for the other things she was into. Things

Charly didn't care to know about, though she had several assumptions.

"You know we could've made a lot of money together," she said to Charly. "But I guess you're more like Lola than I thought. You had me fooled for a second. Running away to make it? Yeah, right! That takes guts." She raked her eyes over Charly. "You got good intentions, but that's all they are. Intentions. You're selfish, Charly. Selfish for not helping me and the community. What you really are is just a small-town girl with big-city dreams, but not the umph to make 'em come true." She revved her engine, looking at Charly with pure disgust in her eyes.

Charly tilted her head and smiled. She'd never seen someone switch personalities so quickly before, and knew for a fact that Nicole was the selfish one. That's why she suddenly hated Charly. She disliked Charly now because she wanted something from her and couldn't get it. That's what Charly had learned from Brigette. She was sugar one second, then turned sour the instant she didn't foresee things going her way.

"I don't see what's so funny," Nicole said. "If I remember correctly, you gave the lady at the desk your last dime, and for what? A stupid dog's vet bill that you'll never be able to fully pay off? Now how you gonna get to New York?"

"You don't know what you're talking about. I haven't even seen a bill," Charly said, knowing there would be one. One she'd really have to make arrangements to pay. She reached into her purse with one hand, then flipped up her middle finger at Nicole with the other. "With this!" she snapped. "I'm going to get to New York with this," she said, looking into Nicole's cold glare with an even icier one. She held up the still brand-new-and-in-the-box Ultra smart Android Nicole had gifted her with. "This has to be worth at least three hundred on the street. Give or take fifty. That's how I'm going to make it!"

# 21

Charly opened her eyes. Her back was aching, her neck was tight and her butt had lost all feeling. She stretched her legs in front of her, wiggled her toes, then remembered she wasn't alone. Hesitantly, she looked up. She was relieved to see the veterinarian clinic was much quieter than it'd been the night before, and there was barely a soul inside. Charly struggled to her feet, grabbed her luggage, then made her way to the counter as if she'd just walked in and hadn't spent the night in the waiting room. A different receptionist greeted her.

"Marlow. I'm here to pick up Marlow," she said, proudly. "I'm Charly St. James. Charly spelled with an L-Y." She quickly closed her mouth. She wanted to get her dog, not kill the receptionist with morning breath.

The receptionist entered something into the computer, then made a weird face, alerting Charly. "Hmm?"

"Hmm?" Charly parroted. "What does hmm mean?"

Her heart began to race and her head shook from side to side. She'd taken all that she could take, and a month ago, would've bet a dollar to a dime that a girl her age was too young to suffer a breakdown. But now she felt herself breaking. She banged on the counter. "Miss? Did you hear me? What does hmm mean?"

The receptionist's eyes bulged, and Charly could see fear pumping in her veins. "I . . . I . . ." she stammered.

"Look, lady," Charly said. "I'm not going to jump on you or curse at you or do anything stupid. I've dealt with enough madness in the last few days, and I wouldn't wish what I've been through on my worst enemy." She rubbed her hand across the counter, then toyed with the business cards in the holder. "I just want to pick up my dog. I brought her in last night, gave you all the money I had on me, and I promise I'll pay it off." She exhaled. "And just yesterday, I lost my home because I won't get rid of her." She nodded. "But I got another one for us."

The receptionist just stared blankly. "I don't know what to tell you. Your dog isn't listed in our system as ever being here, so you don't owe a cent," she said, a bit too chipper for Charly.

Charly blinked slowly as she tried to calm herself. She raised her hand, and was going to hit the counter with every ounce of strength she had, then choke the receptionist until she found Marlow in the computer system. That was the plan. Then her phone vibrated in her pocket and stole her attention. Gave her a second to think. If she choked the lady, she'd go to jail. If she went to jail, she wouldn't see Marlow or New York.

"Shih tzu owner!" a familiar voice called out.

Charly looked to her right, and there stood the veterinarian clinician from the night before. A huge smile spread across her face. He was holding Marlow, who was up and alert. Her tail was wagging. "There she is! But she's not—"

"She's not listed in the computer system," the receptionist interjected. "And I had to tell this young lady, who just lost her home because she won't give up this precious dog, that we didn't have her." She shrugged. "What else do you expect me to do when incompetent people, I swear. . . ." she muttered, finishing her complaint under her breath.

"Let's talk," the guy said, handing Marlow to Charly, then taking an empty seat. He patted the one next to him.

Charly sat. "What's up?" She pet Marlow, then held her up and rubbed noses with her.

"First, Marlow's good. We gave her all her shots, tested her for diseases and worms. She's in excellent condition. She's just so small, so it's easy for her to run her glucose levels down. While she's this little, you should give her a tablespoon of honey. Daily. She's also going to need very nutritious food."

"Okay," Charly said, trying to estimate how much she owed. She didn't know how she was going to do all that.

He scooted to the edge of the seat, rested his elbows on his knees, and clasped his hands together. "She's also one-hundred-percent purebred, and I'm guessing she comes from great genetics. As a breeder, I couldn't help myself. I had to test her. The results will come in later."

Charly nodded.

"In short, you have yourself a show dog. And with the

right training, she could win herself lots of trophies and you lots of money."

Now Charly was curious. Every time someone mentioned money or anything of the sort, she'd been beat. This man was a veterinarian clinician who bred dogs like Marlow in his spare time, so Charly knew he'd want her. But no one could have her. "I know I owe a lot for Marlow's emergency visit—which I promise I'll pay—just like I know the food you say she needs is going to be expensive. I even get that she needs to be supervised because she's so small. But, before you ask, Marlow's not for sale," she said.

The man eyed Charly. "Even though you have no home to take her to?" He tilted his head.

Charly paused. She hadn't expected such a low blow. "I'll get us a home. Don't you worry about that. You just worry about the dogs you need to take care of here, Mr. Vet Worker. For your info, me and Marlow are going to live with my dad's family in New York. I'm going to be a television star and Marlow, thanks to you telling me, will be the best show dog on the planet." Her words were sure, and though she wasn't sure about her dad's family or her and Marlow being famous, she didn't feel like she was lying. Everything she'd said felt truthful. She grinned smugly as if saying, *Take that!* She was now certain that the universe was working in her favor.

Surprisingly, the man smiled and made Charly relax. He nodded. "That's exactly why Marlow isn't in our database, Charly. And it's also why you don't owe us a dime for taking care of her. Last night, I could tell you have the same passion for animals as I did when I was your age. That's why I became a veterinarian and opened my own twenty-four-hour emergency hospital—being a caretaker wasn't enough. I wanted to save animals' lives." He winked.

Her hand was cupped over her face in shame and embarrassment. "I'm sorry. I thought . . ." She shrugged. "I have to pay you more. The shots? The tests? They had to cost you more that I gave last night."

"Don't worry about it, Charly. I donate services to no-kill shelters and kennels all the time. Whatever else you owe, I'll write it off as a donation. He got up, then walked to the counter, beckoning Charly to follow him. He leaned over it, grabbed a pad and pen, then scribbled something on it. He handed it to the receptionist. "Give that to her, will ya?"

The lady smiled. "Sure will. I'll be glad to."

"What's that?" Charly asked.

"Good nutritious food for Marlow, about enough for a week, and a leash to go with the collar we gave her. Oh, and a kennel. If you're traveling, she'll need something to ride in. The prescription is how we prove our donations." He petted Marlow, then patted Charly on her shoulder. "Keep us posted on Marlow's first ribbon. She's gonna win a few." He waved, then disappeared into the back.

Charly stacked Marlow's traveling kennel on top of her luggage, wheeling it out. Her phone vibrated in her pocket. By the time she got everything situated, she saw she had some missed calls. Immediately, she redialed. "Yes?"

"Is this the girl with the dog? The one who gave me the

leash for Petey?" Pee-Wee, the foster child Charly had met, asked.

She wrinkled her brows. She hadn't given her number to Pee-Wee, and, suddenly felt that Nicole was behind the call. Pee-Wee had known who Nicole was, and Charly wasn't sure of the connection. "Yes. How'd you get my number?" she asked.

Pee-Wee laughed. "It was on Petey's collar. You gave him a collar, leash, and Marlow's dog tag. Your name and number's on the back of it."

Charly nodded. She had bought an inexpensive dog tag out of a machine that spit it out almost immediately. And she had listed her name and number in case Marlow had ever gotten lost. "Okay?"

"Well, I just wanted to talk to you." She hesitated. "Well, to warn you, really. You helped me, so I think I should return the favor." Her words came out in a trusting whisper, but Charly wasn't falling for it.

"Let's meet at the nearest bus station. Where's the closest 'Hound to you?" Charly asked, figuring if she couldn't get anything else out of Pee-Wee, she'd at least learn where she and Marlow could depart from once she sold the phone and got bus fare.

"Oh, that's easy. . . ." Pee-Wee began, then gave Charly the address.

# 22

Charly sat in a restaurant across the street from the bus station. Her luggage was in the booth next to her, and Marlow was under the table, asleep in a bag. Her eyes shifted from the big window facing the street to the restaurant customers and employees. She was trying to spot Pee-Wee before Pee-Wee saw her, but it was proving useless. Either the sidewalk in front of the station was too crowded or traffic was too busy for her to see. Still, though, Charly was going to wait her out. She had to see what Pee-Wee was up to, if anything, and she wasn't certain that Nicole wasn't behind the call.

"All you gon' have is water?" a waitress asked in a dry tone, her eyes on an order pad.

Charly looked at the girl, who couldn't have been any older than she. She took her in part by part, starting with her feet. The girl's shoes were dirty, tights too big, and her skirt and sleeves of her blouse had seen better days.

Even though the girl was wearing an apron, Charly could tell her shirt was a mess. Charly bobbed her head. Someone had turned on the music, and it was a song that she knew. An old Chaka Khan hit that DJ used to spin at Smax's. For a second she warmed, thinking about her older friends from home. Wow, she missed them. Smax and his finger waves, Bathsheba and her always pinning money to bras, Rudy-Rudy Double-Duty and his no one can cut corn muffins like you, and Dr. Deveraux El and all his knowledge. Yes, Charly missed them all, but she'd see them when she went back to get Stormy.

"So?" the waitress said, tapping her dirty shoe on the linoleum.

Charly looked at the girl's neck. Ropes and ropes of gold necklaces hung there, way too gaudy for her uniform. Her eyes went up, and she wished she hadn't looked so closely. The girl's hair was awful. Barely able to be pulled back in the ponytail the girl unsuccessfully tried to wear, it jutted here and there, sticking out, haphazardly through a torn hairnet. "You hear that?"

The girl finally looked up from the order pad. "What?"

Charly smiled. "The music."

"Oh, you mean that old mess. I keep telling 'em don't nobody wanna hear that." She looked back down to the pad in her hand. "So, what'chu want?"

Charly didn't know why she did it, but she did. She grabbed the girl's hand. "Listen. If you want to make more money at what you do, I need you to look at me when you talk to me. Be polite . . . even if you have to pretend."

The girl stiffened, then snatched her hand away. "Put your hands on me again, and see what happens. I don't go that way."

Charly's eyes looked at the clock on the wall. She still had fifteen minutes before Pee-Wee was to arrive across the street. She turned her attention back to the girl. She laughed, shaking her head. "Trust me, sweetie. I don't go that way either, and if I did, it wouldn't be you. Not looking like that."

The girl's eyes turned into saucers and her neck snaked. "What?" she asked, dropping the pad to her side. An incredulous look came over her face. "What did you just say?"

Charly, more daring than ever, slid out of the booth. She'd been through so much, and had suffered so much disappointment that she'd learned to expect the worst, and had even prepared for it. She no longer cared. She didn't consider herself crass, just honest. But she was never above helping people, no matter what she'd had to endure. And this waitress needed help. "I said you look a mess." She held up her hands as if surrendering. "I'm not trying to offend you."

"Somebody needs to tell her," another waitress said. The lady was older, around Bathsheba's age, Charly guessed. "These youngins don't know no better 'cause they don't care." She straightened the condiments on another table.

The girl rolled her eyes at the elder waitress. Then she sucked her teeth. "And who are you to tell me anything?" she said to Charly.

Charly perked, and bobbed her head harder as Mary J. Blige's new remake of Chaka Khan's song filled the air. A thick baseline was underneath, making even the elder waitress tap her feet. "I'm Charly. Charly St. James, television star and waitress of the year, three years in a row," she announced, as if it meant anything. She was the only waitress at Smax's who wasn't related to the owners, so she was the only one who qualified to win. Still though, it meant a lot to her.

The girl looked down at Charly's feet. "How are you going to tell me what's wrong with my clothes when you're wearing brown combat boots with red laces? That don't even match."

Charly nodded, then shook her head. "Chocolate. My boots are chocolate. It's all about perception."

"And black striped tights?" the girl asked, eyeing Charly's wide-striped tights.

"Funky. They're absolutely funky," Charly said. "Everything doesn't have to be color-coordinated. Totally matching everything, now that's outdated. Okay? It's okay to be yourself. I'm always myself. Loosen up." She grabbed the girl by the shoulders and moved them up and down. She smiled, then laughed hard and long, still bouncing to the music.

The young waitress finally broke, and a smile widened her face. "You know you were about two seconds from catching a beat-down."

Charly shrugged. "Maybe. Maybe not. There's a lot more to me than meets the eye, so you never know who you're gonna get if you mess with me. And I can tell there's a lot more to you too. Let me give you the game on how to make money in this joint," Charly began, then gave the young waitress the rundown on how to be the best waitress on the planet.

"So, I should dress up? You mean like Halloween?" Her elbows rested on the table now, but she was still standing.

"Yes and no. If Halloween is your thing, yes. If it isn't, no. But fit the atmosphere, make yourself a theme. And don't ever ask a customer 'what'chu want' again . . . unless you don't want tips." Marlow shifted in the bag underneath the booth, and caught both Charly and the waitress's attention. Charly held up a finger to her mouth, then mouthed, *Please, don't tell.*

The waitress raised her brows. "What's that?"

Marlow's head pushed out of the top of the bag, and the girl's eyes widened in fear. "Don't be scared. She's not gonna do anything to you. She's barely three pounds."

"Okay," the waitress calmed herself. "I won't say anything. So, Charly . . . what can I get you on this fabulous day?" she asked, a huge smile on her face.

"Very good. But I only want water." She shrugged. "Me and my puppy here are going to New York, and I don't have money to waste," she said, but thought, *I'm broke.* Her phone vibrated in her pocket, pulling her attention. "One sec," she said to the waitress. Her eyes shifted to the clock on the wall. She had to go. "Hello," she answered Pee-Wee's call.

"I'm almost there," Pee-Wee said. "Meet me in the waiting area by the second set of buses. It's just past a store. . . ." Pee-Wee began rattling directions that made no sense.

"Hold on, Pee-Wee. Let me write this down. You're confusing me." Charly picked up her bag off the floor, trying to keep Marlow out of view of customers and employees, and rifled for paper. She took out her wallet, the Android box, and makeup bag. Finally, she saw something she could write on. Nodding her head, she took down Pee-Wee's directions. "I'm there. I'll meet you in ten." She disconnected Pee-Wee's call, then automatically shot a group text to Stormy, Lola, and Mason, alerting them to her next move. She'd made it a habit to keep them updated. "Done! Sorry. Where were we?" she asked the waitress.

The girl's mouth was on the floor. "Is that the new Android? The one they're calling the Ultra?"

Charly looked at the purse's contents sitting on her lap. Immediately, she began returning things to the bag. She took the Ultra Android box, held it up to her face, then nodded. "Yes."

"But it's not out yet. I've been scouring the Internet looking for it. Saving my money up for it, and they won't even let me preorder it. No preorders until next week, I think." The girl was sitting across from Charly now.

Charly tilted her head. "Really?" She felt the girl's excitement, and knew what she was feeling. She'd been in her shoes, wanting and saving for something, dreaming about it and working for it. "How much is it retailing for? I mean, I know. I'm just curious what the stores are telling you. You know most people can't be trusted," she added, not wanting the girl to be able to one-up her.

"Four-forty-nine with a contract. Seven without. It'll drop after a couple of months, but you already know that," the girl said as if neither price was too high.

"So you're going to wait for it to drop?" Charly asked, knowing the girl's answer would be a direct no. "I mean . . . are you old enough to enter a contract?"

The girl shook her head, and a look of defeat covered her face. "I'm still trying to talk my mom into putting me on her plan. She won't do it, though. I know she won't. So, I've been saving to straight-out buy it. I won't be tied to a contract that way, and can pay month to month."

A huge smile spread Charly's lips. "If you can pay for it today. I'll let you have it for five hundred." She proffered her hand over the table, waiting for the waitress to shake it.

# 23

Pee-Wee had a suitcase in one hand and Petey in the other. Charly's eyes widened. She hadn't expected Pee-Wee to be traveling too, but decided to act like she didn't notice. She couldn't be responsible for anyone else. Getting herself and Marlow to New York was enough worry as it was.

"Hi, Pee-Wee," Charly said, approaching her. She wheeled her bags close to her body so she could keep an eye on Marlow, who she'd put in the carrier.

Pee-Wee stood up and smiled. "Charly!" She let go of her suitcase long enough to give Charly a gentle hug. "I'm so glad to see you."

Charly nodded, her brows high in an okay-for-hugging-me-and-I-don't-really-know-you look. She looked around, a little paranoid, then finally sat. "What's up, Pee-Wee? What can I do for you? And what did you want to warn me about?"

Pee-Wee sat next to her and leaned toward her. "Well, it's about Nicole."

Charly nodded. "I got that on the phone. What is it?"

Pee-Wee looked around, more paranoid than Charly had been. She cut her eyes back to Charly. "You promise not to say anything? I mean nothing. I could get hurt for this."

Charly sensed Pee-Wee was being honest. She was just too scared to be dishonest. She nodded.

"Well, you know the mean girl on the porch. You remember her? The one you were gonna fight?" she blurted in one long breath, then inhaled.

Charly nodded. She had nothing to say. She was here to listen. Listen, then get on a bus to New York. That was it, she had to remind herself.

"Well, that girl works for Nicole. She used to go to stores to check on accounts, to see what people in the community needed. Then she went to schools in a run-down district to see what kind of books they needed. After that, it was clothes, jewelry. You name it." Pee-Wee looked intently into Charly's eyes while she spoke, pausing in just the right places. All Charly could do was nod. "Well, Nicole was roping her in. She gave her everything, material stuff. And the girl was it. I mean I-T it, but then she had to pay Nicole back for all the things she bought and gave her, and the girl never made money because Nicole only paid her in merchandise and room and board. Long story short, Nicole put her on the row."

Charly reared back her head. "The row. I heard Nicole mention that. What is that?" she broke her silence.

Pee-Wee laughed in disbelief. "I guess you ain't from

around here. Think streetwalkers. Nicole takes run-aways, homeless teens—people who don't have anyone else, and she does them wrong. She has money, people who'll do stuff for her. . . ." Pee-Wee gulped. "That's why I just left. I'm moving to Philly."

Charly tilted her head. "What do you mean that's why you left. Nicole did something to you?"

Pee-Wee smiled, then waved a bus ticket in Charly's face. "Because of this, no. But she planned to. She dropped by the other day and asked if I wanted to help her build people and the community. Said all I had to do was find out what people needed so her charity could give it."

Charly nodded, then got up from her seat. "Good for you, Pee-Wee. Go to Philly. Go somewhere." She paused, then remembered what Pee-Wee had told her when they met. She didn't have anyone. "What's in Philly, Pee-Wee? I thought you didn't have family."

Pee-Wee smiled. "Not in the blood sense. But you know what, Charly? Sometimes chosen family is better. I have an older foster sister who lives there, and she told me to come. She aged out of the system when I was twelve, and she'd kept in touch with me ever since. She just graduated college and has a room for me and Petey." She looked at Charly. "And where are you going?"

"New York to find my family," Charly said honestly, remembering she needed to give her aunt a call.

The line for a bus ticket was long, but Charly didn't care. The waitress had come through with the money, and Charly had given her the phone of both of their dreams. A part of her ached for the phone she'd once saved so hard for and left home because of, but now her vision was wider than a smartphone. Her aunt had been happy to hear her voice, and had begged Charly to visit her once she arrived in New York, then made sure that Charly wrote down her address. She'd had so much joy in her voice, Charly was sure she'd let her live with her, but for some reason—probably because she wasn't close with her father's side of the family—she couldn't summon the courage to ask.

"Next!" a woman called from behind the glass.

"A one-way ticket to New York for me and my dog," Charly said, holding up Marlow's kennel to show it to the cashier. This time, she wanted to make sure nothing stopped her from traveling, so she decided to let the bus people know about her canine companion. "Is that okay? I mean, to bring her on the bus."

"If you have her records. Prove she's okay to travel," the lady said, then waved her hand like *child, please*. "Don't worry about it. Just keep her on your lap or on the floor in front of you."

Charly walked down the bus aisle. She had her purse crisscrossed over her shoulder and Marlow's kennel in her hand. All the tension she hadn't even realized she had melted from her shoulders the second her feet connected with the floor. She'd had a hard journey and, possibly, the worst experiences ever. But that was over now, she told herself, settling into a seat located in the middle of the bus. She closed her eyes, ready to sleep and ride, then remembered to power off her phone. As soon as she reached for it, it vibrated. A text from Mason. She shook her head at the thought of leaving him behind. He wasn't really even her boyfriend yet, at least not in a certifiable way, and she'd left him. Now she had to work on keeping him. She just had to figure out how to do it while he was in Illinois and she was in New York. The phone buzzed again because she hadn't checked the message.

MASON: I'll be in NY soon. C u there.

Charly smiled. Yes, she'd see him. She'd see him and find a way to keep him. She wondered if he was bringing Brooklyn along and was powering off the phone when she heard Pee-Wee's voice.

"We get to ride together!" Pee-Wee exclaimed.

Charly looked up, and hoped her not being happy about it hadn't registered on her face. She didn't feel like chitchatting most of the ride. She wanted to sleep. She needed the rest. "Goody," she said, mad at herself for not realizing that Philadelphia was on the way to New York.

Pee-Wee hopped in the seat next to her. "No one's sitting here, right?"

Charly looked at her. "No. But we can't sit together because we both have dogs. Some policy they have," she lied. She didn't want to be mean to Pee-Wee, but she was tired and didn't feel like talking. She wanted to sleep. She smiled. "But it's a good thing you got on when you did. They only allow a certain number of pets on board at a time. You did check Petey in?"

Pee-Wee got up, shaking her head. She hopped in the seat directly across the aisle from Charly. "Nope. But it'll work out. It has to."

Charly shifted her purse until it was wedged between her and the bus, turned Marlow so that she was facing her, then closed her eyes. Pee-Wee may've been taking the ride with her to the Northeast, but that didn't mean she had to talk to her. All she needed to do was dream and plan and plan her dream. New York was only a few stops away, and she intended to be rested enough to deal with it head-on.

# III

## BITING THE BIG APPLE

# 24

"Psst. Charly."

Charly opened her eyes, then cut them to her right. Nothing but faint darkness, passing lights from outside, and a faint glow in the east met her sight. The sun would rise soon. Her head leaned against the bus window, a jacket balled under it serving as her pillow. Punching the fabric to make it more comfortable, she turned her face back toward the open road, then shut her lids again. The ride ahead of her was long, and she wanted to be rested. Marlow moved in her lap, and she put her hand on the kennel to assure her that everything would be okay.

"Psst. Charly."

Charly sat up this time, sure she heard her name. "What?" she whispered. It couldn't be anyone else calling her but Pee-Wee.

Suddenly Pee-Wee plopped down in the seat next to her. "I'm scared, Charly," Pee-Wee admitted and shrugged.

Thunder rumbled and streaks of white light danced in the night sky. Charly rolled her eyes. "Pee-Wee, don't tell me you're afraid of a little rain. You're entirely too old—"

Pee-Wee shook her head. "Not of the rain. I'm afraid of going to Philly, and we're almost there. Can't I just go with you? We could like get a place together. Start a doggy business." She huffed. "I mean, we do have two puppies."

Charly scratched her head. She'd had a hard few days and didn't feel like dealing with Pee-Wee's outlandish dreams. "Look, Pee-Wee, I don't know what to tell you . . . other than we're not supposed to have Marlow and Petey in the same seat. But you know that already." She paused. She was tired and irritated, and was trying to keep it all in check, but Pee-Wee was making it hard. Charly didn't know what it was about Pee-Wee that got under her skin. The girl really hadn't done anything to her. Other than her knowing Nicole, which kept Charly on possible offender alert, Charly had nothing to charge her with. Pee-Wee was just another lost soul seeking to be found. "What do you want me to do, Pee-Wee? I can't just take you to my family's house. I'm trying to piece it all together. I have to land this reality television series, find my dad and get to know him again. You name it, I gotta do it. Look at it this way, at least in Philly, you have stability. Family. But I'll always be a phone call away . . . just in case," Charly added, feeling guilty for being so cut and dry.

"Okay," Pee-Wee said, nodding her head. "Thank you, Charly. Thanks for being just a call away."

Charly looked long and hard at Pee-Wee, then swallowed. Suddenly, she felt sorry for her, and recognized her uneasiness. She was also a little afraid, but she was more scared of going back to her old life. "Just sit here, Pee-Wee," Charly said. "Sit here until we get to Philly." She shrugged, then closed her eyes. "Get some sleep," she said, her lids still shut. "Who cares if two dogs aren't supposed to be so close together on a stupid ride."

It felt like only a few moments had passed before Charly was jolted awake by "We're here, Charly," Pee-Wee said. "Get up. We're here," she repeated.

Charly opened her eyes and stretched. "I see." She gulped, then looked over at Pee-Wee. "Remember what I told you. Don't be afraid. I'm only a call away."

Pee-Wee's arms were around Charly's neck, hugging her. "Thanks, Charly. And I'm here for you, too. Okay? And don't hesitate to call me. We're less than an hour and a half away from each other," Pee-Wee said, squeezing her, then letting go. She got up as the bus pulled into the station, waved, and held Petey in her arms as she made her way down the aisle.

Charly smiled at Pee-Wee's back and wished her the best as she got off the bus and went to start her new life. "Good luck, Pee-Wee," she whispered, then closed her eyes for her less-than-two-hour journey to New York, where she'd capture her dreams.

\*   \*   \*

New York City's Port Authority was on Eighth Avenue and Forty-second Street, and was one of the busiest intersections Charly had ever seen. She walked along Eighth Avenue, her face constantly looking up as she went. Yes, she'd lived outside of Chicago for years, and knew it had its share of tall buildings, but New York was something else. It had a heartbeat, even before nine in the morning. She stopped on the corner of Eighth Avenue and West Forty-first, just opposite of *The New York Times* and a business underneath it called Dean & Deluca. She was amazed that she'd traveled so quickly. Her stomach growled and her mouth was dry. She would've loved to have a cup of coffee and a bagel or a muffin, a couple of the items she saw people carrying out of Dean & Deluca's as she crossed the street, headed to what she assumed was a café. Marlow scratched inside her kennel, and Charly stopped. How was she supposed to grab breakfast with a dog in tow? She looked around as if her answer lay with the busy pedestrians as they walked nine-thousand miles per hour; then a vending cart caught her attention, across a different street. She nodded. She could grab a bite there and, maybe, let Marlow out.

Her feet moved as quickly as the other people's, she noted, keeping pace with the other fast-walking pedestrians as they crossed the street. She was trying to blend in. It was bad enough that she was walking with luggage, she didn't want her greenness to show, proving that she was a tourist. In her mind, she was a bona fide, certified New Yorker, and no one could tell her any different, except for the food vendor.

"Excuse me," Charly asked him, buying a stick of

chicken slathered in barbeque sauce and topped off with a piece of stale bread. "Do you know how to get to Brooklyn?" she asked. She was certain that that's where Mason had said his cousin lived.

The man nodded. "Of course. Who doesn't?" was all he said, continuing to serve customers.

"Well, what about Uptown?" she asked, now with her hand on the corner of his vending stand, hoping for more information. Her aunt had told her that she lived uptown, and Charly believed it was a separate borough of New York like Brooklyn or Queens. She peeked around the opening of the Plexiglas with the menu painted on it in yellow and red. "You know how to get there?"

People whizzed by her, some walking down the street, others up the street. A bunch were crossing at the corner, and one or two stepped directly in front of her as if she weren't standing there and placed their orders. The man served the customers, and paid her no attention. Charly looked around. She'd never seen so many people in her entire life, and she was beginning to feel like New York was going to swallow her whole. "Order something or move it!" the vendor finally spoke.

Charly jumped in front of the next person in line. "Listen. Can you just please tell me how to get uptown?"

Someone laughed behind her. "That's easy. Go uptown." A few people joined in the laughter. A couple others rushed her out of the way. "Little girl, move. We have places to be."

Charly tightened her grip on her luggage, then wheeled her belongings and Marlow out of the way. She kept walking, looking up toward the street signs, watching them climb in numbers. The rude person in the group of people had told her if she wanted to go uptown she had to go uptown, and that's exactly what she was doing. But then her legs started getting tired and her feet began to hurt in the chocolate boots. She shook her head. She'd never have guessed that uptown was so far. Finally, she spotted a line of people sitting. A waist-high cement fence-like structure was just up ahead, and, thankfully, there was room for her.

Plopping down, she unzipped Marlow's kennel, hooked her leash to her collar, then set her on the ground. She closed her eyes for a second to steady herself. She was here. Here in New York, the place of her dreams. So why did she feel so lost? "Don't be helpless," Charly told herself, finally pulling out her phone. She dialed her aunt, but no one answered. She left a voice mail, then decided to contact Mason's cousin that he'd told her about. She couldn't just sit in the city all day, that wasn't helping.

"Hello?" a girl asked. "Who's this?"

Charly gulped. "Um. Hi. This is Charly," she said hesitantly into the phone.

The phone went silent.

"Hello?" Charly said. "Hello?" she looked at her screen to see if the call was still connected.

"Yeah. What do you want? Who are you looking for?" the voice was quick, impatient.

Charly gulped again. She didn't know who she was looking for. Mason hadn't given her a name, only a number. "Well, um . . . I dunno. My friend, Mason, gave me this number—"

"Got'chu. This is Mason's cousin on his mov'vah's side," she said, pronouncing mother more differently than Charly had ever heard. "So, where are you? He said if you called, that meant you needed me. Tell me where you are, and I'll come get you—*but*, it's gonna take me a minute. I mean a real minute. And until I get there, don't talk to nobody. And I mean nobody."

# 25

The sun was higher in the sky. Charly exhaled and wiggled, trying to get her blood circulating. Getting up from the hard concrete slab she'd sat on in downtown Manhattan, on and off, for over three hours, she paced, allowing Marlow some space to roam. They'd done this all day, the waiting, the pacing, the sitting back down and beginning again. Still, though, Charly had waited. She'd phoned Mason, but he didn't answer. He did message her though, then they'd played text tag, and he'd told her to be patient and promised that his cousin was making a way out of no way for Charly, and would be there. He had reassured Charly and she'd believed him.

"Whew," she said to Marlow, then crinkled her brows. Some of the same people Charly had seen passing by her this morning, obviously on their way to work, were now passing back by her on their way to lunch.

"Yo! Girl in the boots?" an odd voice yelled from across the street.

Charly looked around and saw she was the only one in her vicinity who wore boots, then followed the voice. "Me?" she asked, hoping it was Mason's cousin, but not being able to trace the voice.

"Yeah. You. Your name Charly?" a guy asked, sticking part of his upper body out of an SUV's driver's window.

Charly was hesitant to answer. Mason's cousin was female, not male. But the person shouting to her was all guy, and, from where she was standing, he seemed to be alone, but she couldn't be sure of that. The SUV had extremely dark, tinted windows.

"Yo! You Charly or not?" a different voice asked from the back window, which was now rolling down.

A female's soft face appeared, and Charly relaxed. "Yes." She smiled, getting up. "I'm Charly."

Loud music blared from high-end speakers and the guy driving moved his mouth, rapping along with the lyrics. Charly was squashed, wedged between the door and Mason's cousin's hip, but she wouldn't complain. She was off the street and headed toward Brooklyn.

"So how long you here for, Charly?" Mason's cousin asked, wrapping her lips around a bottle of soda, then sipping. She bumped her elbow into the milk crates sitting next to her on the backseat, then cursed under her breath. "Sorry it's so tight in here. My boyfriend deejays, and these are his records. As in real records. He's an old-school spinner, he likes to scratch, but he uses the computer now too."

Charly nodded and smiled. "Hopefully forever," she answered, holding onto the handrail mounted just off the ceiling as the driver took a sharp turn, making her bump into Mason's cousin. "Sorry."

"No problem." Mason's cousin nodded. "So where are we taking you?"

The song turned off and the radio DJ began talking. Charly held up her finger, silencing Mason's cousin. The station was announcing reality show tryouts, and said there were only two days left. "I'm sorry. You were saying?" she asked.

"Where are we dropping you off?"

Charly hadn't realized they were picking her up to drop her off. She thought she was going with them to Brooklyn. "Well, my aunt lives uptown, but works somewhere downtown at the television station . . . where they're filming the reality TV show," she said.

"Cool," Mason's cousin said, not phased by Charly's aunt's job. "So where do you want to go? Uptown or downtown? We're midtown now, so either way is cool with us."

Charly pulled out a piece of paper and looked at her aunt's address. She handed it to the girl. "Here. She lives off Park Avenue."

The girl raised her brows. "Well, this isn't exactly uptown. We're only blocks from this address." She eyed Charly again, then told her boyfriend where to go.

He whistled. "With the kind of paper your aunt must have to live where she lives, I'm surprised she didn't send a limo to pick you up." He shrugged and nodded in the rearview.

Charly watched as sidewalks full of people and tall buildings passed by in a blur. Excitement filled her and made the ride shorter. Finally, the car pulled over to the curb. Charly grabbed Marlow, hopped out, then took her luggage from Mason's cousin, who stood next to her. The girl gave her a quick hug, then hopped back into the backseat of the SUV.

"Take care, and call if you need anything," she said out of the window, then rolled it up. The music turned up, vibrating the windows, and the SUV pulled off into traffic.

Charly waved bye to them from the corner next to her aunt's building and looked at her watch. She would barely have time to shower and change before heading back downtown to audition for the show. She wondered if her aunt could make a call for her so the studio would hold her place. She nodded, sure it was possible. She set Marlow on the ground, then walked toward the black awning where there was a doorman outside waiting.

"Afternoon," he said, opening the door for her and Marlow, then reached for her luggage.

Charly smiled. "No thank you," she said. "I have them." She looked at the piece of paper in her hand, and saw her aunt lived on the top floor.

The doorman raised his eyebrows. "And who are we visiting today, young lady?" he asked, very pleasantly.

"My family." She pointed. "All the way up top."

He nodded, knowingly. "The Michaelses?" he said, looking up, as if thinking. "Yes, that's right. Anniversary time, isn't it? They told me you'd be coming and to let you up. I do apologize, miss. It's been a long day."

Charly pursed her lips together. She remembered Brigette saying something about her aunt getting married years ago and thinking she was too good to take her husband's last name, but for the life of her she couldn't remember if the last name was Michaels or not. She shrugged. If the doorman called them the Michaelses, then that must be their name. "Yes, it is," she said, entering the building and pausing. "This is my first time here in years. Which way do I go?"

He smiled, reaching into his pocket. He pulled out a dog treat and held it up. "Do you mind?" Charly shook her head. He gave it to Marlow. "Glad you asked about the elevators. They're updating the main ones, so I'm afraid you'll have to use service. I do apologize, and please tell Mr. Michaels it won't be long. The service company assured us the elevators would be finished before five." He pointed to the back of the building. "Straight back and to the left, miss. And I must say, you resemble your aunt quite a bit."

Charly turned left and there was a wall straight in front of her with two connecting hallways on either side. She raised her brows and looked down at Marlow.

"Which way do you think we should go?" she asked rhetorically, then decided left would be best. It was, after all, the direction the doorman had given. A person dressed like a janitor walked by them, and Charly assumed she must've selected correctly as the other elevators weren't working. At the end of the corridor was a door, which she opened. Another short hallway was before her, and from what she could see, it opened up to a few rooms. She and Marlow had obviously gone the wrong way. She shrugged, then backtracked until she reached the correct elevator, then hopped on and pressed PH. The elevator didn't budge.

"One second!" the doorman called, then hustled onto the elevator. He stuck a key into the elevator panel and turned it. "Glad I caught you. Sorry, this one won't go up to the penthouse without a key. Enjoy your day, miss."

Soft jazz greeted her ears when the elevator doors opened. Her eyes bulged. She had been expecting another hallway, but instead she was inside her aunt's apartment. "Just like TV," she said, stepping off. "Hello?" she called out, walking through the huge, immaculate apartment, which didn't resemble her idea of an apartment at all. It looked more like the first floor of a mansion. "Hello? It's me, Charly. . . ." she called again, and only heard her voice float with the music.

Walking through the place, Charly grew more and more impressed. Her aunt had really made something for herself, and Charly assumed being a hotshot at the network must've paid well because her aunt lived like a queen. Either that, or she'd married up. She wheeled her bags while Marlow walked beside her. Charly looked on the wall, saw that it was almost noon.

"We gotta hurry, Marlow," Charly said, then zipped through the apartment until she found a bathroom. She had to hurry and shower, then get down to the auditions before they closed.

# 26

The line of people waiting to audition snaked around the corner and all the way down the block. Charly walked next to the line, guessing there had to be hundreds of people ahead of her. She overheard someone saying that people had showed up as early as the night before. She gripped Marlow's leash in her hand, continuing to put one foot in front of the other, as if she was only walking the dog.

"Move it," a cop said, keeping the crowd in check.

Charly eyed him, then smiled.

"Move it," he said to her, then pointed the other way. "And go back that way. The line's back there."

She gulped. New Yorkers were tough. At home she could've gotten away with what she was up to, but not here. And, she told the cop, the only thing she was doing was checking out who was going to be on the next number-one reality TV show—*and looking for a way to sneak in so*

*I can be one of the headliners*, she thought, crossing the street. The cop couldn't tell her she couldn't walk down the other side of the block. The people auditioning were numerous, and had shown up in much larger numbers than she'd thought, she realized when she reached the corner and walked head-on into some station interns.

"Can you believe these people think they're all gonna get seen today? We've endured at least five hundred since this morning," a girl began, then caught sight of Marlow. "Oh. My. Gosh. She's just the cutest," she said to Charly. "I've been wanting a shih tzu for like forever."

"Huh. I bet'cha she's better than that terror, Sugar," an intern muttered.

Charly stopped, letting the first intern play with Marlow. She smiled to herself, thinking her dog was better than Sugar, whoever Sugar was. "Thanks. Yes, shih tzus are sweethearts," she said to the girl, trying to hear what the other intern was saying about Sugar, then noticed the conversation dwindling off. "Sorry, but we've got to go. There are too many people around here for her to concentrate on using it. Sorry again," she apologized to the girl, seeing that the other interns were walking away. Charly needed to see which direction they were going in, but didn't want to follow them because she didn't want to alert them. "Say bye to the nice lady, Marlow," she said to Marlow, then pretended to be walking her.

The group of interns crossed the street, walking in the opposite direction of the line. They walked in front of the building, passed it, then turned. *Going through a side door*, Charly noted, running to catch up and see them, she hoped, before one of them spotted her. With just a second to spare, she noticed them open a door, then enter. She looked at her watch. She didn't know how she was going to do it, but, somehow, she'd fit Marlow into her audition. And if that didn't work, she had plan B—the side door the interns had just disappeared into. She turned to walk away, then was stopped by a familiar name.

"Sugar! Stop it!"

Charly turned and saw a small black dog running toward her and Marlow. She couldn't tell what kind of dog it was, but it was fast and out of control.

"Sugar! I. Said. Stop," a young lady yelled. She wore a college T-shirt, a pair of jeans, and slip-on shoes. "Please, stop her!"

Charly looked around, and realized that Ms. College was talking to her. She shrugged, then turned toward a barreling Sugar, and squatted. She put Marlow between her thighs, then held out her hands for Sugar, who ran into them with no problem.

"Oh, thank you," the girl said, out of breath. "There is just no controlling this one. If you hadn't have stopped her, Mr. Day would've fired me over his Sugar. You'd think controlling a show would help you control your pet, but no . . ."

Sugar gripped Charly by the throat. So Sugar belonged to the creator of the reality television series? She nodded, noticing the girl had an all-access pass around her neck. "No problem," she said and picked Sugar up and handed her to the girl.

Sugar leaped in the air. Both Charly and the other girl reached to catch her before she hit the ground. Suddenly,

Charly's legs were in the air and her butt was off the ground. Around her ankle was Marlow's leash.

"Oh!" the other girl said, covering her mouth as Charly's backside collided with the sidewalk.

"Ouch! Ugh!" Charly grimaced between gritted teeth, not knowing how she'd gotten caught in Marlow's leash. She was in so much pain, she was sure it'd take minutes to get up.

Marlow whined, licking Charly's hand.

"Oops. Thanks!" the girl said, then grabbed Sugar and jetted down the block toward the intern entrance.

Charly shook her head. The least the girl could've done was make sure that she was okay. At the rate her pain was stabbing her, she was sure she wasn't going to make the audition. "Come on, Marlow," she said, crawling to her knees, then forcing herself up. With step after step of pain, she finally made it back around the corner to the line. Before she got to the end of it, she saw the crowd start to disperse. Auditions were off for the day. She shook her head, then headed back the way she came. She was too hurt to walk, and she didn't want to get lost in the crowd. Charly figured the fastest way to a cab was the empty side of the block.

"Oh," she said, when she sat on almost the exact spot that her butt had connected with the ground. Sugar's walker, rude as she was, had left a gift for Charly, the girl just didn't know it. On the ground was her all-access pass. It wasn't on the band, but it was there.

"Back so soon?" the doorman greeted her when she and Marlow got out of the cab.

Charly nodded, gripping a bag of junk food and drinks she'd purchased from the nearby deli, then set Marlow on the ground. "Yes. I'm glad too. It's been a long day," she said, wanting to add, "And I need to get some food and rest," but thought better of it. She walked into the building with the doorman on her heels. He beat her to it and turned the key to allow her access to her aunt's, and Charly zipped to the penthouse.

When the doors opened, the scent of food lingered in the air and relief moved through her. It felt so good to be home, even if her aunt hadn't said she could live there, and she couldn't wait to eat and lie down. Stepping off the elevator, she kicked off her boots and headed to the bedroom where she'd left her luggage. Opening the door, she exhaled, set Marlow on the bed, and immediately began disrobing. It was nice to have her own bathroom, she thought, discarding her clothes on the way. Down to her panties and bra, she entered the bathroom and turned on the shower.

"Who are you?" a lady's voice asked.

"It's me. . . ." Charly turned, then almost jumped out of her skin. She'd never seen the woman before, and assumed she must be the maid. "Sorry, I'm Charly. My aunt knows I'm here."

The lady reared back her head and put her hands on her hips. "Who is your aunt?"

Charly huffed. Clearly the maid needed an attitude adjustment. "Your boss. My aunt owns this place."

The lady's eyebrows and voice rose. "*I* own this apartment, and I don't know you or your aunt. You have one minute to get out, or I'm calling the cops."

# 27

Charly got off the elevator two floors below. She knew by now that the lady, whoever she was, had alerted security and, probably, the doorman. Hustling down the hallway, she dug in her purse for her phone. She was sure she had the correct address, and could've kicked herself for not walking through the entire apartment before heading to the television audition. But she hadn't had time. Her heart raced and she shook in the boots she'd barely had time to put on. Her eyes searched for an exit sign as her fingers dialed Stormy.

"Stormy," she yelled in a loud whisper. "Have you heard from Auntie?" She spotted a sign that said STAIRS, then jogged to it, clutching Marlow in the same hand she held her phone and wheeling her luggage behind her.

"No. I left a couple of messages, but she hasn't called back yet. I guess she's still at work," Stormy said. "Why do you sound so out of breath?"

Charly pushed through the exit door, then stood in the stairwell while she updated Stormy on the happenings. Leaning against the wall, she caught her breath. There was no way she could talk to her sister and walk down the stairs quietly. Her hands were too full.

"So what are you gonna do? Can you call Mason's cousin back? Maybe she can pick you up."

Charly shook her head no. "Yes, that's what I'm gonna do, Stormy," she lied. There was no way she was going to call Mason's cousin back. If she wanted a ride, she'd hail one. That seemed to be the only thing Mason's family was going to offer her, and she couldn't blame them. They didn't even know each other. Charly didn't even know the woman's name. "I'm going to call her after I call Mason. He's supposed to be coming here."

"Un-uhn," Stormy said. "I wouldn't count on it. At least not for a week or so. His mom is sick."

Charly kicked her heel against the wall. "Okay. It's no problem. I'll call or text you later and let you know what's up. And I'll keep trying Auntie. You do the same." She hung up with Stormy and made her way down flight after flight of stairs, then cracked a door leading to the fourteenth floor. Carefully, she looked both ways before entering the floor completely, and saw the hall was empty. Her heart still drummed in her chest, and she could hear its beat in her ears and back of her throat. Exhaling, she made her way to the service elevator located off an almost hidden nook at the end of the hall. She guessed people with a lot of money didn't have to be bothered with the sight of the help's transportation to their floor, and she was thankful for it. Tucked away in a recessed part of the apartment building, it had allowed her to travel to the basement without being seen.

The doors opened without so much as a ding, and Charly held her breath for a second and listened. Not a sound met her ears. She poked out her head, looked left and right, and not a soul was in sight. She nodded, gripped her luggage and tugged on Marlow's leash, then stepped off. She passed several doors, and, to her dismay, all of them were locked. Finally, at the end of the hall, she saw one with a sign on it that read PRIVATE. Charly shrugged, then wrapped her hand around the doorknob and tried to turn it. It didn't move. She shook her head. Just like all the others, it was locked, and she wasn't surprised. In a building such as the one she was in, she didn't expect anything to be unsecure. Marlow whined, then tried to dart down the hall. Charly planted her feet firmly on the ground, but almost tripped over Marlow's leash. She grabbed the knob to help keep her balance, and the door eased opened.

"Huh!" she said. The door was locked, but it wasn't closed all the way.

The room was dark. Pitch black and eerie, but Charly didn't care. She needed a place to sleep, and it was either here or on the street. Closing the door behind her and Marlow, she felt on the wall for a light switch, then perked. She pushed a button and the room came to life. She was in a good-sized storage room. Boxes with apartment numbers lined a wall, shelves were on another, and holiday decorations were tucked here and there. Charly walked through the room, taking in everything and trying to see where she and Marlow would sleep. She turned a corner she hadn't seen when she first entered, and her shoulders relaxed a bit. There was an old dusty cot along the wall that looked as if it hadn't been used in forever. "Yes," she said, when she made her way over to it, and patted her hand on it. A cloud of dust rose, telling her that no one had slept here in a long while, and she knew she was safe for the night. She turned and almost jumped in the air in glee. A tiny bathroom, barely big enough to be a broom closet, opened off the room. It had a toilet and sink, and that was all she needed.

She went on a scavenger hunt, digging in boxes until she found something to cover the cot with and something she could sleep under. In a box marked XMAS, she found a long gold ribbon, and two ceramic candy bowls, which she filled with water and the food the veterinarian had given her. Still rifling through the storage space, she found paper for Marlow to go potty and an outlet to charge her phone. Then she opened all the sweets she'd purchased from the store earlier, and ate them for dinner.

# 28

The morning came without event. At least, Charly thought so. The storage room had no windows, so she couldn't really be sure what time it was. She turned on her side, then coughed. A billow of dust rose, and she waved it away. She reached for her cell phone, pressed the button, and looked at the clock. She had plenty of time to get ready for auditions. Rolling to a sitting position, she put her feet on the floor. Her boots met it with a thump. She'd slept in her clothes.

Marlow stirred next to her. Charly had kept her on the cot with her. There was no way she was going to let Marlow sleep on the floor. For all she knew, there could be rats down there. She was in New York, after all.

Her phone buzzed in her hand—a text from Stormy had come through while she was asleep. It said to call her aunt. Charly exhaled. She'd forgotten all about calling her aunt, though she had remembered to keep her promise to

Stormy, and she'd texted her a lie saying that she was spending the night over Mason's cousin's house, then had curled up and called it a night.

"Hello, Auntie?" Charly asked when an early-morning voice greeted her ears. It was raspy, so it was hard to tell to whom it belonged.

"Charly? Charly, is that you?" her aunt asked.

"Yes. I'm here. I'm here, and you told me to call you when I got here," she rattled, "but you never answered."

Her aunt laughed. "Slow down, Charly. You talk a mile a minute just like your dad. If I didn't answer, that means I was at work, baby. Now tell me, where's here?"

"New York. In the city," Charly informed, still whispering and petting Marlow.

Again, her aunt laughed. "I know that, Charly. But *where* are you in New York? It's a big city." A train sounded in the background, followed by a strong breeze.

"Manhattan. But where are you? I went by your apartment, and they said you didn't live there. I went by . . . one second," she said, fishing in her purse for the paper with the address on it. She found it, then read the address off to her aunt.

Her aunt laughed. "Close, but wrong. I don't live on Park Avenue. I live just *off* Park Avenue. Park Avenue in *Harlem*. Harlem is still Manhattan. . . . I'll explain later. Right now I'm on my way to work. Just tell me where you are, and I'll meet you there when I get off. Or you can meet me there."

She was in a cab and headed to the audition before she knew it. Her pulse was still racing, and she didn't know how she'd gotten past the doorman, but she did. The cabbie zipped through traffic, punching on his brakes every couple of minutes, making Charly's head jerk. Her stomach turned from all the swerving and braking, but she wouldn't complain.

He swerved and stopped. "Here good enough?" he asked, pressing on the meter.

Charly took some money out of her pocket, paid him, and hopped out. "Keep the change," she said, gripping Marlow with one arm and shaking her luggage handle until she freed it from where it was lodged in the back seat. "Yes," she said, setting Marlow on the ground, then reaching into her purse, and hanging the all-access pass around her neck that was hanging on the gold Christmas ribbon she'd found while searching the storage room.

She turned the corner, walking quickly down the street. Marlow trotted next to her like the perfect little dog, and Charly couldn't have been more thankful. The entrance was in front of her before she knew it. Charly gulped back the anxiousness that was rising in her chest, reached for the door, and said a silent prayer. She hadn't expected it to open, but it did. Adjusting the pass around her neck, she walked down the busy hall, trying to avoid all eye contact. She needed to blend in.

"Hey, you. Girl with the dog and luggage," a voice said.

Charly kept moving. "Can't," she said, without turning around. "I gotta go get Sugar. She's scheduled for socialization training today," Charly lied to whoever it was, walking straight ahead and sneaking quick looks into open doors as she passed them. She had no idea where

Sugar was, but she'd find out. She'd find her, then figure out what to do next. She didn't really have a plan.

Footsteps followed after her. "Wait a second," the same voice said.

Charly held her breath, then stopped and turned around. She came face-to-face with a guy a bit older than her, who looked like he'd been dipped in caramel. Tall and lanky, he had the brightest brown eyes she'd ever seen and a prominent mole on the right side of his chin.

"Yes?" she asked; then her eyes widened when he took off his baseball hat. "Oh," slipped out of her mouth, and she could've kicked herself. His hair was a shock of gray.

"Genetic," he explained. "So what are you doing with the bags?" he asked. "If you're here to socialize the monster, why the luggage?"

Charly was quick with her lie. "Socialization. First I'm going to let her and this puppy play together, then introduce her to other dogs and people in the park. After that, we're going to work on socializing her with objects around. Mr. Day wants Sugar to be able to travel through the airport and not run from rolling baggage."

The guy smiled and nodded. "Makes sense. You can just put the luggage in the room down the hall, last door on the right, until you need it," he said, then turned around.

Major relief swept through Charly. She walked down the hall as fast as she could without dragging Marlow, and found the room the guy had told her about. In a flash, she'd almost thrown her luggage inside, and was on her way back out into the hall to find the audition room, but then something caught her eye. He'd told her to store her bags in Sugar's area, she discovered when her eyes met the doggy playpen, toys, bowls of food and water, and a potty area lined with training pads. Charly picked up Marlow. "I'm sorry, baby," she said, setting her in the playpen. "But I promise I'll be right back. I gotta go win us a spot on this reality television show series."

QUIET: AUDITION IN PROGRESS met Charly's eyes when she turned the corner. There, lined up against the wall, were some of the interns she'd seen the day before. Charly smiled, then stuck the all-access badge in her shirt. The girl who'd played with Marlow was there.

"Where are you coming from?" she asked, then stopped. She eyed Charly carefully. "Don't I know you?"

Charly nodded. "From yesterday."

The intern raised her brows. "The girl with the dog." She looked Charly up and down suspiciously, then her eyes landed on Charly's boots. "Brown combat boots. Red shoestrings." She looked at the other interns, who nodded, making Charly uncomfortable.

Charly tilted her head. "Yes . . . why?"

The girl shook her head. "It's just different. A good look though. So . . ."

A different intern walked up on the group, clutching a clipboard to her chest. "Are you one-zero-three-four?" she asked Charly.

"Um," Charly began. "Yes."

The intern nodded. "Well, it's about time. I was calling your number. You almost lost your spot."

"Bathroom," Charly lied.

"In there," the intern pointed, then followed behind Charly as she entered the door.

"Number one-zero-three-four," the girl said, then walked out of the room.

A blond lady with a pleasant smile gestured for Charly to sit. "Have a seat. Tell me about yourself."

Charly stammered. She was ready to audition, not divulge her life story. "I thought this was an audition. This is where I try out for the new television show, right?" she asked, making sure to keep a smile on her face and sound as sweet as she could.

The lady nodded. "Well, yes and no. This part is the interview. There's no real way to audition someone for a reality show, you know."

Charly nodded, then exhaled. She tried to tell herself to calm down, that everything was going to be okay. "My name is Charly St. James. I'm sixteen—"

"Why don't you tell us where you're from, and how much you went through to make it to this interview?" a man's voice said from behind. "Just keep looking straight ahead. Talk into the camera."

"Um . . . um," Charly stammered again. *You can do this. You can.* "Well, I'm from Illinois. I came here by bus, train . . . you name it—"

The woman's eyes widened and her cheeks flushed.

"Let's skip to how you got inside the building through the employee entrance."

Charly was going to die. She felt her heart stop beating, then its thump slowing down in her ears until it became an almost nonexistent thud . . . thud . . . thud.

"Huh?" she finally said, then turned around. "Oh.

God." There in front of her was the man with the shocking gray hair.

He proffered his hand to her. "Nice to meet you, Charly St. James. I'm Mr. Day, the creator of this show and Sugar's owner. I must say, I've never met anyone who wanted something so badly."

Charly shrugged. "That's because you hadn't met me. Let me reintroduce myself. My name is Charly. Charly St. James, television star."

# Epilogue

Charly sat on the sofa next to Stormy stuffing her face with popcorn. Marlow lay across her lap, curled up, asleep.

"You excited?" Stormy asked.

Charly nodded. She was excited. So ecstatic she didn't know what to do with herself. Mr. Day had cast her, had said he loved her determination and drive, had called her a good girl who lived in a bad girl, but the deal wouldn't be sealed until one of her parents signed the contract.

"You're going to be just fine," her aunt said, coming into the room and taking a seat on the chair next to the sofa. "Look at everything that has happened so far. Your life is what you make it, Charly."

Stormy elbowed her, nodding. "Yep. You see I'm here, thanks to you."

Charly nudged her sister back. "That's only 'cause

Brigette wanted to go to Jersey to hit the casinos. And I still had to find a way to pay for her trip."

"But at least it got me here for the weekend. At least I'm here for your big day," Stormy added. "Now we just gotta get you back in school."

Charly shook her head, then shrugged. Mr. Day's crew had convinced Brigette to enroll Charly in a public online school. "I am in school. I just don't have to physically go to class—"

A knock on the door shut Charly up.

Her aunt shot her a look, then got up to answer it.

"Ready?" Stormy asked, then added, "You know Mason will be here tomorrow?"

Charly nodded yes to both of Stormy's questions. "As ready as I'll ever be."

"Your future begins now," her aunt said, opening the door.

Charly jumped out of her seat, ran to the door, and took a deep breath. On the other side of the door, one of her biggest wishes turned inside out, until it became truth. She'd come to New York to capture her dreams with an S. She wanted to be on television, and she wanted to see her father.

"Daddy?" she said, then a huge smile spread on her face.

*Stay tuned for Charly's next epic fiasco!*

# CHARLY'S EPIC FIASCOS

## Kelli London

## ABOUT THIS GUIDE

The following questions are intended to
enhance your group's reading of
CHARLY'S EPIC FIASCOS.

# Discussion Questions

1. At age sixteen Charly moved away from home to fulfill her dreams and better herself. Considering the situation, was she too young? Why/why not?

2. Charly and Stormy were very close. Did Charly betray her sister by leaving her in such a bad situation or did she do the right thing by going ahead and paving the way for them both?

3. Theft is theft, and no one has the right to steal from another person, not even that person's parent. Should Charly have turned in Brigette to the cops for stealing her money or was she right in giving Brigette a pass because she's her mother?

4. Brigette and Grandma Anna stole from Charly, and neither woman was right for doing so. However, Charly jumped a turnstile (which is considered stealing from the transit system) and "saved" Marlow, the dog that rightfully belonged to someone else despite what the original owner had planned for Marlow's life. Was Charly wrong or did the circumstances demand it and, therefore, change immoral into moral?

5. Why do you think Charly lied to Mason so much? Is lying ever appropriate? Why/why not?

6. Have you been in an overwhelming situation that caused you to become tongue-tied and/or lie about your actions to make you fit in? Is there ever a good reason to become or pretend to be something you're not?

7. Charly encountered some colorful people on her journey and learned that some people aren't necessarily who you believe them to be. However, Charly was lucky. Her desperateness could've led to danger. Could Charly have formed a safer plan?

8. There's an old cliché that when things seem too good to be true, they usually are. Where and how did this cliché fit into Charly's journey, and how could she have learned from it earlier?

9. Charly has trust issues. She couldn't trust her mother, the characters who "helped" her out on her journey, or, oftentimes, her own judgment. Do you think she'll be able to trust her father? Would you?

COMING SOON!

*Hollywood High*

by Ni-Ni Simone and Amir Abrams

Welcome to Hollywood High, where socialites rule
and popularity is more of a drug than designer digs
could ever be.

# 1

# London

Listen up and weep. Let me tell you what sets me apart
from the rest of these wannabe-fabulous broads.

I *am* fabulous.

From the beauty mole on the upper-left side of my
pouty, seductive lips to my high cheekbones and big,
brown sultry eyes, I'm that milk chocolate–dipped beauty
with the slim waist, long sculpted legs, and triple-stacked
booty that had all the cuties wishing their girl could be
me. And somewhere in this world, there was a nation of
gorilla-faced hood rats paying the price for all of this gor-
geousness. *Boom*, thought you knew! Born in London—
hint, hint. Cultured in Paris, and molded in New York,
the big city of dreams. And now living here in La-La
Land—the capital of fakes, flakes, and multiple plastic
surgeries. Oh . . . and a bunch of smog!

Pampered, honey-waxed, and glowing from the UMO
24-karat gold facial I just had an hour ago, it was only

right that I did what a diva does best—be diva-licious, of course. So, I slowly pulled up to the entrance of Hollywood High, exactly three minutes and fifty-four seconds before the bell rang, in my brand-new customized chocolate brown Aston Martin Vantage Roadster with the hot pink interior. I had to have every upgrade possible to make sure I stayed two steps ahead of the rest of these West Coast hoes. By the time I was done, Daddy dropped a check for over a hundred-and-sixty grand. Please, that's how we do it. Write checks first, ask questions later. I had to bring it! Had to serve it! Especially since I heard that Rich—Hollywood High's princess of ghetto fabulousness—would be rolling up in the most expensive car on the planet.

Ghetto bird or not, I really couldn't hate on her. Three reasons: a) her father had the whole music industry on lock with his record label; b) she was West Coast royalty; and c) my daddy, Turner Phillips, Esquire, was her father's attorney. So there you have it. Oh, but don't get it twisted. From litigation to contract negotiations, with law offices in London, Beverly Hills, and New York, Daddy was the powerhouse go-to attorney for all the entertainment elite across the globe. So my budding friendship with Rich was not just out of a long history of business dealings between my daddy and hers, but out of necessity.

Image was everything here. Who you knew and what you owned and where you lived all defined you. So surrounding myself with the Who's Who of Hollywood was the only way to do it, boo. And right now, Rich, Spencer, and Heather—like it or not—were Hollywood's "It Girls." And the minute I stepped through those glass doors, I was about to become the newest member.

Heads turned as I rolled up to valet with the world in the palm of my paraffin-smooth hands, blaring Nicki Minaj's "Moment 4 Life" out of my Bang & Olufsen BeoSound stereo. I needed to make sure that everyone saw my personalized tags: LONDON. Yep, that's me! London Phillips—fine, fly and forever fabulous. Oh, and did I mention . . . drop dead gorgeous? That's right. My moment to shine happened the day I was born. And the limelight had shone on me ever since. From magazine ads and television commercials to the catwalks of Milan and Rome, I may have been new to Hollywood High, but I was *not* new to the world of glitz and glamour, or the clicking of flashbulbs in my face.

Grab a pad and pen. And take notes. I was taking the fashion world by storm and being groomed by the best in the industry long before any of these Hollywood hoes knew what Dior, Chanel, or Yves Saint Laurent stood for: class, style, and sophistication. And none of these bitches could serve me, okay. Not when I had an international supermodel for a mother, who kept me laced in all of the hottest wears (or as they say in France, *haute couture*) from Paris and Milan.

For those who don't know. Yes, supermodel Jade Phillips was my mother. With her jet black hair and exotic features, she'd graced the covers of *Vogue*, *Marie Claire*, *L'Officiel*—a high-end fashion magazine in France and ninety other countries across the world—and she was also featured in *TIME*'s fashion magazine section for being one of the most sought out models in the industry. And now she'd made it her life's mission to make sure I follow in her diamond-studded footsteps down the cat-walk, no matter what. Hence the reason why I forced myself to drink down that god-awful seaweed smoothie, compliments of yet another one of her ridiculous diet plans to rid me of my dangerous curves so that I'd be runway ready, as she liked to call it. Translation: a pro-truding collarbone, flat chest, narrow hips, and a pan-cake flat butt—a walking campaign ad for Feed the Hungry. *Ugh!*

I flipped down my visor to check my face and hair to make sure everything was in place, then stepped out of my car, leaving the door open and the engine running for the valet attendant. I handed him my pink canister filled with my mother's green gook. "Here. Toss this mess, then clean out my cup." He gave me a shocked look, clearly not used to being given orders. But he would learn today. "Umm, did I stutter?"

"No, ma'am."

"Good. And I want my car washed and waxed by three."

"Yes, ma'am. Welcome to Hollywood High."

"Whatever." I shook my naturally thick and wavy hair from side to side, pulled my Chanels down over my eyes to block the sparkling sun and the ungodly sight of a group of Chia Pets standing around gawking. Yeah, I knew they saw my work. Two-carat pink diamond studs bling-blinging in my ears. Twenty-thousand-dollar pink

Hermès Birkin bag draped in the crook of my arm, six-inch Christian Louboutin stilettos on my feet, as I stood poised. Back straight. Hip forward. One foot in front of the other. Always ready for a photo shoot. Lights! Camera! High Fashion! Should I give you my autograph now or later? *Click, click!*

# 2

# Rich

The scarlet-red bottoms of my six-inch Louboutins gleamed as the butterfly doors of my hot pink Bugatti inched into the air and I stepped out and into the spotlight of the California sun. The heated rays washed over me as I sashayed down the red carpet and toward the all-glass student entrance. I was minutes shy of the morning bell, of course.

Voilá, grand entrance.

An all-eyes-on-the-princess type of thing. Rewind that. Now replace princess with sixteen-year-old queen.

Yes, I was doin' it. Poppin' it in the press, rockin' it on all the blogs, and my face alone—no matter the headline—glamorized even the cheapest tabloid.

And yeah, I was an attention whore. And yeah, ummhmm, it was a dirty job. Scandalous. But somebody had to have it on lock.

Amen?

Amen.

Besides, starring in the media was an inherited jewel that came with being international royalty. Daughter of the legendary billionaire, hip-hop artist, and ground-breaking record executive, once known as M.C. Wickedness and now solely known as Richard G. Montgomery Sr., president and C.E.O. of the renowned Grand Records.

Think hotter than Jay-Z.

Signed more talent than Clive Davis.

More platinum records than Lady Gaga or her monsters could ever dream.

Think big, strong, strapping, chocolate, and handsome and you've got my daddy.

And yes, I'm a daddy's girl.

But bigger than that, I'm the exact design and manifestation of my mother's plan to get rich or die trying—hailing from the gutters of Watts, a cramped two-bedroom, concrete ranch, with black bars on the windows and a single palm tree in the front yard—to a sixty-two thousand square foot, fully staffed, and electronically gated, sixty acre piece of 90210 paradise. Needless to say, my mother did the damn thing.

And yeah, once upon a time she was a groupie, but so what? We should all aspire to be upgraded. From dating the local hood rich thugs, to swooning her way into the hottest clubs, becoming a staple backstage at all the concerts, to finally clicking her Cinderella heels into the right place at the right time—my daddy's dressing room—and the rest is married-with-two-kids-and-smiling-all-the-way-to-the-bank history.

And sure, there was a prenup, but again, so what? Like

my mother, the one and only Logan Montgomery, said, giving birth to my brother and me let my daddy know it was cheaper to keep her.

Cha-ching!

So, with parents like mine my life added up to this: my social status was better and bigger than the porno-tape that made Kim Trick-dashian relevant and hotter than the ex-con Paris Hilton's jail scandal. I was flyer than Beyoncé and wealthier than Blue Ivy. From the moment I was born, I had fans, wannabes, and frenemies secretly praying to God that they'd wake up and be me. Because along with being royalty I was the epitome of beauty: radiant chestnut skin, sparkling marble brown eyes, lashes that extended and curled perfectly at the ends, and a five-foot-six, brick house thick body that every chick in L.A. would tango with death and sell their last breath to the plastic surgeon to get.

Yeah, it was like that. Trust. My voluptuous milkshake owned the yard.

And it's not that my stuff didn't stink, it's just that my daddy had a PR team to ensure the scent faded away quickly.

Believe me, my biggest concern was my Parisian stylist making sure that I murdered the fashion scene.

I refreshed the pink gloss on my full lips and took a quick peek at my reflection in the mirrored entrance door. My blunt Chinese bob lay flush against my sharp jawline and swung with just the right bounce as I confirmed that my glowing eye shadow and blush was Barbie-doll perfect and complemented my catwalk-ready ensemble.

Black diamond studded hoops, fitted red skinny leg jeans, a navy short-sleeve blazer with a Burberry crest on the right breast pocket, a blue and white striped camisole, four strands of sixty-inch pearls, and a signature Gucci tote dangled around my wrist.

A wide smile crept upon me.

*Crèmedelacrème.com.*

I stepped across the glass threshold and teens of all shapes and sizes lined the marble hallways and hung out in front of their mahogany lockers. There were a few newbies—better known as new-money—who stared at me and were in straight fan mode. I blessed them with a small fan of the fingers and then I continued on my way. I had zero interest in newbies, especially since I knew that by this time next year, most of them would be broke and back in public school throwing up gang signs. Okay!

Soooo, moving right along.

I swayed my hips and worked the catwalk toward my locker, and just as I was about to break into a Naomi Campbell freeze, pose, and turn, for no other reason than being fabulous, the words, "Hi, Rich!" slapped me in the face and almost caused me to stumble.

*What the . . .*

I steadied my balance and blinked, not once but four times. It was Spencer, my ex-ex-ex-years ago-ex-bff, like first grade bff—who I only spoke to and continued to claim because she was good for my image and my mother made me do it.

And, yeah, I guess I'll admit I kind of liked her—sometimes—like one or two days out of the year, maybe. But

244 Ni-Ni Simone and Amir Abrams

every other day this chick worked my nerves. Why? Because she was el stupido, dumb, and loco all rolled up into one.

I lifted my eyes to the ceiling, slowly rolled them back down, and then hit her with a smile. "Hey, girlfriend."

"Hiiiiii." She gave me a tight smile and clenched her teeth.

Gag me.

I hit her with a Miss America wave and double-cheeked air kisses.

I guess that wasn't enough for her, because instead of rolling with the moment, this chick snatched a hug from me and I almost hurled. Ev'ver'ree. Where.

Spencer released me and I stood stunned. She carried on, "It's so great to see you! I just got back from the French Alps in Spain," She paused. Tapped her temple with her manicured index finger. "Or was that San Francisco? But anyway, I couldn't wait to get back to Hollywood High! I can't believe we're back in school already!"

I couldn't speak. I couldn't. And I didn't know what shocked me more: that she put her hands on me, or that she smelled like the perfume aisle at Walgreens.

*OMG, my eyes are burning . . .*

"Are you okay, Rich?"

*Did she attack me?*

I blinked.

*Say something . . .*

I blinked again.

*Did I die . . . ?*

*Say. Something.*

"Umm, girl, yeah," I said, coming to and pinching myself to confirm that I was still alive. "What are you wearing? You smell—"

"Delish?" She completed my sentence. "It's La-Voom, Heather's mother's new scent. She asked me to try it and being that I'm nice like that, I did." She spun around as if she were modeling new clothes. "You like?" She batted her button eyes.

*Hell no.* "I think it's fantast!" I cleared my throat. "But do tell, is she still secretly selling her line out of a storage shed? Or did the courts settle that class action lawsuit against her for that terrible skin rash she caused people?"

Spencer hesitated. "Skin rash?"

"Skin to the rash. And I really hope she's seen the error of her . . . ways. . . ." My voice drifted. "Oh my . . . wow." I looked Spencer over, and my eyes blinked rapidly. "Dam'yum!" I said tight-lipped. "Have you been wandering Skid Row and doing homeless boys again—?"

"Homeless boys—?" She placed her hands on her hips.

"Don't act as if you've never been on the creep-creep with a busted boo and his cardboard box."

"How dare you!" Spencer's eyes narrowed.

"What did I do?!" I pointed at the bumpy alien on her neck. "I'm trying to help you and bring that nastiness to your attention. And if you haven't been entertaining busters, then Heather's mother did it to you!"

"Did it to me?" Spencer's eyes bugged and her neck swerved. "I don't go that way! And for your information, I have never wandered Skid Row. I knew exactly where I was going! And I didn't know Joey was homeless. He lied and told me that cardboard box was a science experiment. How dare you bring that up! I'm not some low-level hoochie. So get your zig-zag straight. Because I know you don't want me to talk about your secret visit in a blond wig to an STD clinic. Fire crotch. Queen of the itch, itch."

My chocolate skin turned flaming red, and the South Central in my genes was two seconds from waking up and doing a drive-by sling. I swallowed, drank in two deep breaths, and reloaded with an exhale. "Listen here, Bubbles, do you have Botox leaking from your lips or something? Certainly, you already know talking nasty to me is not an option, because I will take my Gucci-covered wrist and beat you into a smart moment. I'm sooo not the one! So I advise you to back up." I pointed my finger into her face and squinted. "All the way up."

"You better—"

"The only commitment I have to the word better, is that I *better* stay rich and I *better* stay beautiful, anything other than that is optional. Now you on the other hand—what you *better* do is shut your mouth, take your compact out, and look at the pimple face bearrilla growing on your neck!"

She gasped.

And I waited for something else nasty to slip from her lips. I'd had enough. Over. It. Besides, my mother taught me that talking only went thus far, and when you tired of the chatter, you were to slant your neck and click-click-boom your hater with a threat that their dirtiest little secret was an e-mail away from being on tabloid blast.

"Now, Spencer," I batted my lashes and said with a tinge of concern, "I'm hoping your silence means you've discovered that all of this ying-yang is not the move for you. So, may I suggest that you shut the hell up? Unless, of course, you want the world to uncover that freaky blue video-taped secret you and your mother hope like hell the Vatican will pray away."

All the color left her face and her lips clapped shut.

I smiled and mouthed, "Pow! Now hit the floor with that."

# 3

# Spencer

I can't stand Rich! That bug-eyed beetle walked around here like she was Queen It when all she really was, was a mess! I should've pulled out my crystal nail file and slapped her big face with it. Who did she think she was?

I fanned my hand out over the front of my denim mini-dress, shifting the weight of my one-hundred-and-eighteen-pound frame from one six-inch, pink-heeled foot to the other. Unlike Rich, who was one beef patty short of a Whopper, I was dancer-toned and could wear anything and look fabulous in it. But I *chose* not to be over-the-top with it because unlike Rich and everyone else here at Hollywood High, *I* didn't have to impress anyone. I was naturally beautiful and knew it.

And yeah, she was cute and all. And, yeah, she dressed like no other. But that ho forgot I knew who she was *before* Jenny Craig and *before* she had those crowded teeth shaved down and straightened out. I knew her when she was a chunky, bucktooth Teletubby running around and losing her breath on the playground. So there was no way Miss Chipmunk wanted to roll down in the gutter with me 'cause I was the Ace of Spades when it came to messy!

I shook my shoulder-length curls out of my face, pulled out my compact, and then smacked my Chanel-glossed lips. I wanted to die but I couldn't let pie-face know that, so I said, "Umm, Rich, how about *you* shut *your* mouth. After all the morning-after pills you've popped in the last two years, I can't believe you'd stand here and wanna piss in my Crunch Berries. Oh, no, Miss Plan B, *you* had better seal your own doors shut, *first*, before you start tryna walk through mine. You're the reason they invented Plan B in the first place."

I turned my neck from side to side and blinked my hazel eyes. *Sweet . . . merciful . . . kumquats!* Heather's mother's perfume had chewed my neck up. I wanted to scream!

Rich spat, "You wouldn't be trying to get anything crunked would you, Ditsy Doodle? You—"

"OhmyGod," London interrupted our argument. Her heels screeched against the floor as she said, "Here you are!" She air-kissed Rich, then eyed me, slowly.

*Oh, no, this hot-buttered beeswax snooty-booty didn't!*

London continued, "I've been wandering around this place all morning . . ." She paused and twisted her perfectly painted lips. "What's that smell?" London frowned and waved her hand under her nose, and sniffed. "Is that, is that you, Spencer?"

"Umm-hmm," Rich said. "She's wearing La-Voom,

from the freak-nasty-rash collection. Doesn't it smell del-ish?"

"No. That mess stinks. It smells like cat piss."

Rich laughed. "Girrrrl, I didn't wanna be the one to say it, since Ms. Thang wears her feelings like a diamond bangle, but since you took it there, *meeeeeeeeow*!"

The two of them cackled like two messy sea hens. Wait, hens aren't in the sea, right? No, of course not. Well, that's what they sounded like. So that's what they were.

"I can't believe you'd say that?!" I spat, snapping my compact shut, stuffing it back into my Louis Vuitton Tribute bag.

"Whaaaaatever," London said, waving me on like I was some second-class trash. "Do you, boo. And while you're at it. You might want to invest in some Valtrex for those nasty bumps around your neck."

I frowned. "*Valtrex?* Are you serious? For what?"

She snapped her fingers in my face. "Uh, hellllllo, Space Cadet. For that nastiness around your neck, what else? It looks like a bad case of herpes, boo."

Rich snickered.

I inhaled. Exhaled.

Batted my lashes.

*Looks like I'm going to have to serve her, too.*

I swept a curl away from my face and tucked it behind my ear.

Counted to ten in my head. 'Cause in five . . . four . . . three . . . two . . . one, I was about to set it up—wait, wait, I meant set it off—up in this mother suckey-duckey, okay? I mean. It was one thing for Rich to try it. After all, we've *known* each other since my mother—media giant and billionaire Kitty Ellington, the famed TV producer and host of her internationally popular talk show, *Dish the Dirt*—along with Rich's dad, insisted we become friends for image's sake. And in the capital of plastics, appearance *was* everything. So I put up with Rich's foolery because I had to.

But, that chicken-foot broad, London, who I only met over the summer through Rich, needed a reality check—and *quick*, before I brought the rain down on her. Newsflash: I might not have been as braggadocious as the two of them phonies, but I came from just as much money as Rich's daddy and definitely more than London's family would ever have. So she had better back that thang-a-lang up on a grill 'cause I was seconds from frying her goose. "You know what, London, you better watch your panty liner!"

She wrinkled her nose and put a finger up. "Pause."

*Did she just put her finger in my face?*

"Pump, pump, pump it back," I snapped, shifting my handbag from one hand to the other, putting a hand up on my hip. My gold-and-diamond bangles clanked. "You don't *pause* me, Miss Snicker-Doodle-Doo. I'm no CD player! And before you start with your snot ball comments, get your facts straight, Miss Know It All. I don't own a cat. I'm allergic to them. So why would I wear cat piss? And I don't have herpes. Besides, how would I get it around my neck? It's just a nasty rash from Mrs. Cummings' new perfume. So that goes to show you how much you know. And they call me confused. Go figure."

"You wait one damn minute, Dumbo," London hissed.

*"Dumbo?!* I'll have you know I have the highest GPA in this whole entire school." I shot a look over at Rich, who was laughing hysterically. "Unlike some of *you* hyenas who have to buy your grades, *I'm* not the one walking around here with the IQ of a Popsicle."

Rich raised her neatly arched brow.

London clapped her hands. "Good for you. Now . . . like I was saying, *Dumbo,* I don't know how you dizzy hoes do it here at Hollywood High, but I will floor you, girlfriend, okay. Don't do it to yourself."

I frowned, slammed my locker shut. "Oh . . . my . . . God! You've gone too far now, London. That may be how *you* hoes in New York do it. But we don't do that kind of perverted nastiness over here on the West Coast."

She frowned. *"Excuse* you?"

I huffed. "I didn't stutter, Miss Nasty. I *said* you went too damn far telling me not to do it to myself, like I go around playing in my goodie box or something."

Rich and London stared at each other, then burst into laughter.

I stomped off just as the homeroom bell rang. My curls bounced wildly as my stilettos jabbed the marbled floor beneath me. *Welcome to Hollywood High,* trick! *The first chance I get, I'm gonna knock Miss London's playhouse down right from underneath her nose.*

But first, I had more pressing issues to think about. I needed to get an emergency dermatologist appointment to handle this itchy, burning rash. My heels scurried as I made a left into the girls' lounge instead of a right into homeroom. I locked myself into the powder room. I had to get out of here!

OMG, there was a wildfire burning around my neck. *Ooooh, when I get back from the doctor's office, I'm gonna jumpstart Heather's caboose for her mother trying to do me in like this.*

I dialed 9-1-1.

The operator answered on the first ring, "Operator, what's your emergency?"

Immediately, I screamed, "Camille Cummings, the washed-up drunk, has set my neck on fire!"

# 4

# Heather

My eyes were heavy.
Sinking.

And the more I struggled to keep them open, the heavier they felt. I wasn't sure what time it was. I just knew that dull yellow rays had eased their way through the slits of my electronic blinds, so I guessed it was daylight.

Early morning, maybe?

Maybe . . . ?

My head was splitting.

Pounding.

The room was spinning.

I tried to steady myself in bed, but I couldn't get my neck to hold up my head.

I needed to get it together.

I had something to do.

*Think, think, think . . . what was it . . .*

*I don't know.*

*Damn.*

I fell back against my pillow and a few small goose feathers floated into the air like dust mites.

I was messed up. Literally.

My mouth was dry. Chalky. And I could taste the stale Belvidere that had chased my way to space. No, no, it wasn't space. It was Heaven. It had chased my way to the side of Heaven that the crushed-up street candy, Black Beauty, always took me to. A place where I loved to be . . . where I didn't need to snort Adderall to feel better, happier, alive. A place where I was always a star and never had to come off the set of my hit show, or step out of the character I played: Wu-Wu Tanner. The pop-lock-and-droppin'-it fun, loving, exciting, animal-print wearing, suburban teenager with a pain in the butt little sister, an old dog, and parents who loved Wu-Wu and her crazy antics.

A place where I was nothing like myself—Heather Cummings. I was better than Heather. I was Wu-Wu. A star. Every day. All day.

I lay back on my king-sized wrought-iron bed and giggled at the thought that I was two crushed pills away from returning to Heaven.

I closed my eyes and just as I envisioned Wu-Wu throwing a wild and crazy neighborhood party, "You better get up!" sliced its way through my thoughts. "And I mean right now!"

I didn't have to open my eyes or turn toward the door to know that was Camille, my mother.

The official high blower.

"I don't know if you think you're Madame Butterfly, Raven-Simoné, or Halle Berry!" she announced as she moseyed her way into my room and her matted mink slippers slapped against the wood floor. "But I can tell you this, the cockamamie bull you're trying to pull this morning—"

*So it was morning.*

She continued, "Will not work. So if you know what's best for you, you'll get up and make your way to school!"

*OMG! That's what I have to do! It's the first day of school.*

My eyes popped open and immediately landed on my wall clock: 10:30 A.M. It was already third period.

I sat up and Camille stood at the foot of my bed with her daily uniform on: a long and silky white, spaghetti-strap, see-through nightgown, matted mink slippers, and a drink in her hand—judging from the color, it was either brandy or Scotch. I looked into her glassy blue eyes. It was Scotch for sure. She shook her glass and the ice rattled. She flipped her honey blond hair over her blotchy red shoulders and peered at me.

I shook my head. God, I hated that we resembled. I had her thin upper lip, the same small mole on my left eyelid, her high cheekbones, her height: five-foot-six, her shape: busty: 34D, narrow hips and small butt.

Our differences: I looked Latin, although I wasn't. I was somewhere in between my white mother and mysterious black father. My skin was Mexican bronze, or more like a white girl baked by the Caribbean sun. My hair was Sicilian thick and full of sandy brown coils. My chocolate eyes were shaped like an ancient Egyptian's. Slanted. Set in almonds. I didn't really look white and I definitely didn't look black. I just looked . . . different. Biracial—whatever that was. All I knew is that I hated it.

Which is why, up until the age of ten, every year for my birthday I'd always blow out the candles with a wish that I could either look white like my mother or black like my father.

This in-between thing didn't work for me. I didn't want it. And I especially didn't like looking Spanish when I wasn't Spanish. And the worst was when people asked me what was I? Where did I come from? Or someone would instantly speak Spanish to me! WTF! How about I only spoke English! And what was I? I was an American mutt who just wanted to belong somewhere, anywhere other than the lonely middle.

Damn.

"Heather Suzanne Cummings," Camille spat as she rattled her drink and caused some of it to spill over the rim. "I'm asking you not to try me this morning, because I am in no mood. Therefore, I advise you to get up and make your way to school—"

"What, are you running for PTA president or something?" I snapped as I tossed the covers off of me and stood to the floor. "Or is there a parent-teachers' meeting you're finally going to show up to?"

Camille let out a sarcastic laugh and then she stopped abruptly. "Don't be offensive. Now shut up." She sipped her drink and tapped her foot. Her voice slurred a little.

"I don't give a damn about those teachers' meetings or PETA, or PTTA, PTA, or whatever it is. I care about my career, a career that you owe me."

"I don't owe you anything!" I walked into my closet and she followed behind me.

"You owe me everything!" she screamed. "I know you don't think you're hot because you have your own show, do you?" She snorted. "Well, let me blow your high, missy—"

*You already have . . .*

She carried on. "You being the star of that show is only because of me. It's because of me and my career you were even offered the audition. I'm the star! Not you! Not Wu-Wu! But me, Camille Cummings, Oscar award-winning—"

"Drunk!" I spat. "You're the Oscar award-winning and washed-up drunk! Whose career died three failed rehabs and a million bottles ago—!"

*WHAP!!!!*

Camille's hand crashed against my right cheek and forced my neck to whip to the left and get stuck there.

She downed the rest of her drink and took a step back. For a moment I thought she was preparing to assume a boxer's position. Instead, she squinted her eyes and pointed at me. "If my career died, it's because I slept with the devil and gave birth to your evilness! You ungrateful little witch. Now," she said through clenched teeth as she lowered her brow, "I suggest you get to school, be seen with that snotty nose clique. And if the paparazzi happens to show up, you better mention my name every chance you get!"

"I'm not—"

"You *will*. And *you will* like it. And *you will* be nice to those girls and act as if you like each and every one of them, and especially that pissy princess Rich!" She reached into her glass, popped a piece of ice into her mouth, and crunched on it. "The driver will be waiting. So hurry up!" She stormed out of my room and slammed the door behind her.

I stood frozen. I couldn't believe that she'd put her hands on me. I started to run out of the room after her, but quickly changed my mind. She wasn't worth chipping a nail, let alone attacking her and giving her the satisfaction of having me arrested again. The last time I did that it took forever for that story to die down and besides, the creators of my show told me that another arrest would surely get me fired and Wu-Wu Tanner would be no more.

That was not an option.

So, I held my back straight, proceeded to the shower, snorted two crushed Black Beauties, and once I made my way to Heaven and felt like a star, I dressed in a leopard catsuit, hot pink feather belt tied around my waist, chandelier earrings that rested on my shoulders, five-inch leopard wedged heels, and a chinchilla boa tossed loosely around my neck. I walked over to my full-length mirror and posed. "Mirror, mirror, on the wall, who's the boom-boom-flyest of 'em all?" I did a Beyoncé booty bounce, swept the floor, and sprang back up.

The mirror didn't respond, but I knew for sure that if it had, it would've said, "You doin' it, Wu-Wu. You boom-bop-bustin'-it fly!"

# HAVEN'T HAD ENOUGH? CHECK OUT THESE GREAT SERIES FROM DAFINA BOOKS!

## DRAMA HIGH

by L. Divine

Follow the adventures of a young sistah who's learning that life in the hood is nothing compared to life in high school.

| THE FIGHT | SECOND CHANCE | JAYD'S LEGACY |
|---|---|---|
| ISBN: 0-7582-1633-5 | ISBN: 0-7582-1635-1 | ISBN: 0-7582-1637-8 |
| FRENEMIES | LADY J | COURTIN' JAYD |
| ISBN: 0-7582-2532-6 | ISBN: 0-7582-2534-2 | ISBN: 0-7582-2536-9 |
| HUSTLIN' | KEEP IT MOVIN' | HOLIDAZE |
| ISBN: 0-7582-3105-9 | ISBN: 0-7582-3107-5 | ISBN: 0-7582-3109-1 |
| CULTURE CLASH | COLD AS ICE | PUSHIN' |
| ISBN: 0-7582-3111-3 | ISBN: 0-7582-3113-X | ISBN: 0-7582-3115-6 |

| THE MELTDOWN | SO, SO HOOD |
|---|---|
| ISBN: 0-7582-3117-2 | ISBN: 0-7582-3119-9 |

## BOY SHOPPING

by Nia Stephens

An exciting "you pick the ending" series that lets the reader pick Mr. Right.

| BOY SHOPPING | LIKE THIS AND LIKE THAT | GET MORE |
|---|---|---|
| ISBN: 0-7582-1929-6 | ISBN: 0-7582-1931-8 | ISBN:0-7582-1933-4 |

## DEL RIO BAY

by Paula Chase

A wickedly funny series that explores friendship, betrayal, and how far some people will go for popularity.

| SO NOT THE DRAMA | DON'T GET IT TWISTED | THAT'S WHAT'S UP! |
|---|---|---|
| ISBN: 0-7582-1859-1 | ISBN: 0-7582-1861-3 | ISBN: 0-7582-2582-2 |

| WHO YOU WIT? | FLIPPING THE SCRIPT |
|---|---|
| ISBN: 0-7582-2584-9 | ISBN: 0-7582-2586-5 |

## PERRY SKKY JR.

by Stephanie Perry Moore

An inspirational series that follows the adventures of a high school football star as he balances faith and the temptations of teen life.

| PRIME CHOICE | PRESSING HARD | PROBLEM SOLVED |
|---|---|---|
| ISBN: 0-7582-1863-X | ISBN: 0-7582-1872-9 | ISBN: 0-7582-1874-5 |

| PRAYED UP | PROMISE KEPT |
|---|---|
| ISBN: 0-7582-2538-5 | ISBN: 0-7582-2540-7 |